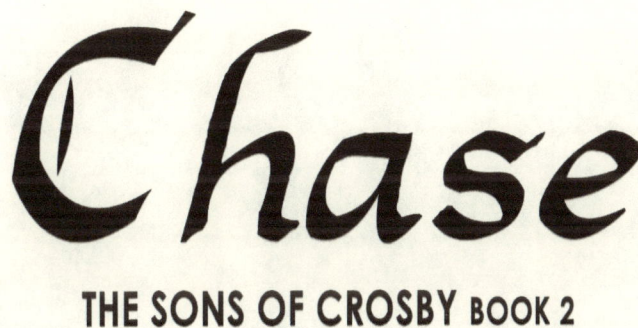

THE SONS OF CROSBY BOOK 2

KATHI S. BARTON

This is a work of fiction. Names, characters, places, and incidents are products of the author's imagination or are used fictitiously and are not to be construed as real. Any resemblance to actual events, locations, organizations, or persons, living or dead, is entirely coincidental.

World Castle Publishing, LLC
Pensacola, Florida
Copyright © Kathi S. Barton 2017
Paperback ISBN: 9798891264038
eBook ISBN: 9781629898513
First Edition World Castle Publishing, LLC, December 11, 2017
http://www.worldcastlepublishing.com
Licensing Notes
Cover: Karen Fuller
Editor: Maxine Bringenberg

Chapter 1

Chase put the book down on his desk and thought about what he'd just read. He'd been doing that a great deal lately, reading about the woman that was still in his freezer. She had been hard to figure out, what she was and how she'd come to be, but Kilian had come to his rescue just yesterday and had helped him a great deal. Not that he still didn't have a million questions, but for the most part, he did have a better understanding and knowledge of what she was.

"Do you have a question I can answer for you, Lord Chase?" He told Spud, a friend of Jewel, that he didn't know, what he wanted to ask right now. "Understandable. The lady queen, she has put someone in charge of watching over her. There are few who didn't want to be here, but she has picked a couple to help you as well. The helper is called Sunshine. She will be here as long as the Lady Warrior is."

Chase had found out that while Emerald was very powerful and old, she wasn't an ice dragon, but the protector of them. Yes, she was created in ice, but had the appearance of a human in all ways. It was so she would to be able to withstand the heat should there be a need, but her job was to fight with and to protect dragons, dragons made entirely of ice. And not just any ice either, but ice so cold that it was as hard as stone, which would only melt when the heat from the sun shone directly on them for one thousand years. He'd never heard of such a thing.

"Where is her dragon, do you know?" Sunshine, his new helper, bowed before him and told him that she was looking for him now. "So, is he dead or alive? Or don't you know that yet?"

"I believe him to be dead, my lord, but I can't be sure just yet. Forgive me for not having the answer right now." He told Sunshine that he didn't expect her to have them all right now, but to keep looking. "I am, my lord. We all are. To have an ice dragon alive would be a great thing."

He didn't know why but he let it go. To his way of thinking, to have a full-sized dragon around would be scary. But then he hadn't ever met a dragon, so he wasn't sure what full sized could mean. To him they were great creatures that smashed houses. For all he knew they could be no bigger than the faerie in front of him.

Emerald had been in his freezer for a week now. She'd come out on occasion, stare at him or whoever was in the room with him, then go back inside. Her sword was always drawn, and she was covered from head to toe in ice…her shield, he'd been told. He'd also read that she would be cold at all times, much like someone that was dead. He didn't want to think about that too much.

The rest of his day was spent trying to catch up on some paperwork. He'd moved all his office — well, most of it — into the kitchen when going back and forth between there and his actual office was too time consuming. Besides, he thought that it was working out better anyway, as he seemed to be getting more done than sitting in his office, staring at the wall.

Dad had been making it to his house about suppertime every night since he'd been told that Chase had his mate. It had been both wonderful and nerve-wracking at the same time. He loved his dad, more than anything, but he asked too many questions and in a small space of time. And that was what made him tense about this entire thing, not having the answers when his dad assumed that he should.

As soon as he walked in the door, Chase put up his hand. "No, I've not spoken to her. Yes, she's still in there. No, I've not learned anything more than I did yesterday, and no, I'm not going to go in there and see if she needs me. She's fine where she is." Dad sat down, but looked to be a little miffed. "Dad, I'm scared enough without you adding to my already overflowing cup of what ifs."

"Can't a man be curious about his newest family member?" Chase said that he could, so long as he didn't ask him about her. "You think she's going to be all right in there after all this time?"

"No, I think she's dead and I'm only waiting until you leave before I go in, wrap her in a thick blanket, and bury her in the back yard." His dad growled. "Dad, I don't know anything about her other than she worked for Jewel, knows a lot of languages, and that someone, someone deadly, is after her."

"There are a lot of people around town that don't belong here, so you know. And Jason has talked to a few of the people in your mate's neighborhood, who said that Emerald has helped them out a bit, so they don't tell them anything." He said that Jason had told him that last night. "He said that he's got some people watching those guys in the hotel too. I thought that you should know that they're not moving around much during the day, mostly in the evening, asking questions.

I think they figure that people would be more respective of a few questions after they've had dinner. Morons."

"Are they human?" Dad told him that a few of them were, but they were wolves for the most part. "Do you know if they've registered with the pack leader? That could be an easy way to check them out."

"They're by the books, I can tell you that. Donald said that not only had they come to him to tell them that they were here, but they gave him some story about being here on a shopping expedition. To put in a plant of some kind. I don't know what that would be, and Donald said he can't ask." Yeah, Chase knew that as well. They had to report to him if they were wolf, but not tell him why they were here other than to say it was business or vacation. "He said to tell you that he has his men and women working in the hotel that they're in, and they have been snooping around."

"I hope they're being careful. These men don't seem the sort to mess with." Dad said that they were being extra careful, as they seem to have suspicious minds as well. "What do you mean? They figure someone is looking into their lives?"

"Said that while they're in the rooms—cleaning up, you know—there seems to be a lot of luggage, and most of it is locked up. They can't tell, like one of us can, what's in there, but they don't bother them. One of them told Donald that they could smell silver in the cases, so were kind of afraid to touch them." Dad looked around then back at him, and Chase found himself leaning in to hear what he had to say. "I've been in their rooms...not so they'd see me, but in there. They have all kinds of equipment that I had to ask what it was when I got back. Jewel is helping me find out what it is, but mostly it's lab equipment. And a big saw. Like them kind that you'd have when felling trees for a house."

"To remove my head." They both stood when Emerald

8

came out of the freezer and spoke. "I've healed for the most part, but I now need to feed."

Chase felt his own body's need to feed overwhelm him. Sitting down, he tried to calm himself and his beast. It wasn't working. He needed her, they both did. When she moved by him to the sink, he growled low and she paused to look at him.

"You've been here for more than a week, and I've not been able to feed either. I'm sorry. I don't want to rush you or scare you, but just letting you know." She nodded and poured herself a glass of juice, juice that he knew for a fact hadn't been in his refrigerator before she'd opened it. "You know what I am to you."

"My mate. I'm not sure how that works with you being a vampire, but I'm not an easy person to know. I'm a loner as well." She drained the glass of juice then poured herself another. The next time she drained it, it filled on its own. "What is it you expect from me?"

It was on the tip of his tongue to tell her to come sit on his naked cock. To let him have her in a very carnal way. But he only looked at her, hoping to Christ that not only could she not read his mind, but that she wasn't as dangerous as he'd heard she could be. Then he realized that he'd not answered her yet.

"Expect? Nothing that you're not willing to give me. Answers would be great, but having the questions in any kind of order or even coherent right now isn't going to happen. I've been reading up on what I could find, or someone has given me. I know a little about your kind, but that's it, just a little." She asked him what he wanted to know. "You're a warrior. Where is your dragon?"

"He died some decades ago. More than I care to think about." He nodded and told her that he had figured that was

9

what she'd say. "I was harmed when he was taken off the field we were fighting on. He died later, from other wounds. Not that it matters, but the people who are looking for me now, the ones chasing me, they think that I can tell them things about why I've been alive for so long. Something about pictures from long ago. I don't think that they know what I am. But that hasn't stopped them from trying to find me. It's been hard to keep away; they must have resources that are good. But I can't let them capture me for any reason, because that would cause a lot of creatures a great deal of trouble. Including you. And if I won't give them what they want, then they'll simply remove my head."

"They have lab equipment with them. And as you said, a saw to remove your head. I'm thinking, unlike you, that they know just what you are and what you could bring to them if they were to capture you." She didn't say anything, but sat at the table he and Dad were at. "What can we do to protect you? I'm assuming that somewhere along the line, you've trusted people before who betrayed you. I won't. Never. And neither will my family."

"As I have been told before. Sorry, but my levels of trust don't include you just yet. That doesn't mean that I won't eventually, but for now, I don't." She didn't elaborate, and he didn't ask. If he was honest, he wasn't even sure he wanted to know. "You are the son of Crosby, the vampires that saved the Queen Kilian."

"Yes, and you are Emerald, dragon warrior, rider and protector of the ice dragons and last female of your kind." She nodded, and he could see her shifting under the façade of clothing that she had worn when she'd come out of the freezer. "You're magical, the most magical creature that has ever lived, too."

"Yes, and by being my mate, you are as well." He had

10

already figured that would happen, but it didn't make it any easier for him to question her. "You will be safe with me, Chase Crosby. This I can promise you with my sword."

~~~

Kilian was excited and afraid to meet the warrior. She knew who she was, of course. All creatures of the earth knew who the great Emerald was. But when she entered the dwelling that housed her, she knew immediately that while she was healed, she was still very weak. Looking at Chase as he sat with her at the table, Kilian wondered if he knew that she was just as hungry as he was.

"I've come to bless you with some of my magic." Kilian had only come to talk to the warrior, but knew that she was going to need more than she was getting right now. "My lady, you need to feed, and soon. I'm sure that you're aware of this, but you're unwell."

"I'm all right. I've been talking to the vampire here." She nodded at Chase and he smiled. Kilian loved this young man—because he was to her, young—more than she did any of the others. Which was saying a great deal, as she loved them all very much. But Chase had a heart of gold, and he was as kind a person as she'd ever met. "He has it in his head that he's going to protect me. I don't need protecting from a vampire, or any other creature that comes to this house. So we're coming to an understanding, he and I. He'll let me do my job and not get in my way."

"You do need him, however." Emerald looked at her, and Kilian could see that she was angry. At who or what she didn't know, but she bowed before her. "You need only to tell him and Chase will help you."

"He cannot, and you know this." Kilian said that she knew no such thing, and looked at the warrior when she laughed. "The vampire isn't going to be—"

"Chase. Say it...my name is Chase, Chase Crosby." He grinned, and Kilian wondered if he knew how much more handsome he was when he did that. "You have to stop calling me *the vampire*, as that isn't something about me that a great many people know. Chase. You can say it in several languages, I'm sure."

"It would be all the same, as well you know. But there are things that you don't understand. You can't get close to me, vampire. I am a danger to not just you, but to all mankind if they find me. Especially here." He asked her why here. "You are here. So is your family."

"Yes, so they are. And for what it's worth, they'd help me in any kind of way that you needed. But as for the men in town that are here for you, I can tell you right now, they have no idea where you are, or that you've healed. Nor do they know exactly what we'll do to them when they try anything. As I said before, we're a tight family of vampires, with magic that none others have. Also, we can call on many other packs and leaps at any time. *They* like us." She asked him why he thought that they'd not get to her. "Because, I have taken care that they don't. And we have people working in the building that they're in who are watching their every move. Even what they eat and what they send back to the kitchen. Did you know that they don't drink anything but water? Why is that, I wonder? It could be that they, like me, don't care for sugary drinks, but who knows? But they like water."

"So, they aren't human." Kilian laughed when Chase told her no shit. "I'm not one to fuck with. I have a great deal riding on me staying alive."

"Yes, you do, and so do I. I have my life and everything that I am riding on you staying alive." He stood up and Kilian marveled at his height, as she did all the Crosby boys when she was near them. "My brothers and I are working very hard

12

on keeping you safe, and have been since you were put into my freezer to heal. We've all taken turns in making sure that you were taken care of, that you had all that you needed, and that no one, at least only those that we trust, knew where you were. As far as anyone knows, they haven't any idea that you've been in my freezer all this time."

When Emerald stood up as well, Kilian decided that she'd come to talk to the warrior some other time, and slipped out of the house as quietly as she'd entered. She found herself smiling at nothing when she made her way back to her home.

There were going to be fireworks when those two came together, and Kilian was glad that she was close enough to see them when they did. The Crosbys were a powerful group of men, but they paled considerably when their magic was put against one as strong as the warrior. Chase was going to be a vampire to be reckoned with, more so than he was now.

"My queen?" She looked at Sunshine and allowed her to speak freely. She found this rule, as old as she was, the most annoying of all of them. To have to ask to speak to her. "We have located the body of the ice dragon, my lady. Three, as a matter of fact. They have been dead for a great many years. His body, like that of two others, has been hidden within the caves of the mountain. By the same hand, we believe. They have not been bothered, my lady. Their bodies are still as they had been when they entered. No human has ever touched them. Not in all these years."

"The ice warrior, you think she put them in there?" Sunshine nodded. "How did they perish? Were you able to ascertain that?"

"Yes, my lady. Two of the dragons were very old and worn out. They wished to die and did so. They have been moved and put to rest in the gardens here. I hope that is all right with you. The cave they were found in, it was not proper

13

for ones such as them. Her dragon, the ice warrior's, he was killed by his own hand. She brought him to the cave to be with his family in his last moments, I think. But he ended his life on his own." Kilian asked how they were related. "His parents, my lady. Both his mother and father were put there by the warrior, as well as several, smaller dragons that were killed by war. The dragon of the ice warrior, he had been hurt badly when he was hidden away. He finished himself to free her of his life."

He had been her true dragon, and Emerald should have died with him…her heart having beat with his. But since he killed himself—the only thing he could do for her to be free to move on—her life did not end with his. As soon as he died, by his own hand, it separated their hearts. Her heart would beat for only Chase now. It was the thing that Kilian might have done, should she have been a dragon for a warrior.

"How do you know this? That he died by his own hand?" Kilian was handed a thick slab of stone, hand cut and a great many years old. She read the accounting of the incident then looked at Sunshine. "Have you told anyone of this?"

"No. I was to tell his lordship, Lord Chase, but I thought you should know first." She nodded. This changed so many things for them. "He gave her his all, my lady. All that they were, even his parents, was gifted to the warrior for her service to them. This is a great thing he did for her. And the title that is now hers."

The king and queen of the dragons had been found, it seemed. After all these many years, their bodies had been found, and Kilian was both saddened by their deaths and happy that someone had taken care that their bodies were safe. She herself had looked for them whenever she was out and about, the earth not giving her their whereabouts, and now she knew why. Emerald had hidden them away so that their forms could be safe. For all of them.

"Tell the Crosbys that I wish to speak to them. All of them. And the warrior. She might know what her dragon has done for her, but I have my doubts. But I have to let them all know what this means. Not just to Chase and Emerald, but to the family as a whole. There will be others now that will come for her, and when they do, there will be hell to pay." Sunshine asked if she could be paired with the warrior. "You will need to ask her, my child. And do not be surprised if she tells you no. Her life has been hard since she was created, and I doubt she has had a friend or helpmate at all since then."

"I will await your conversation with them before I put the question to her." Kilian thought that a good idea. "She is the queen of the warriors as well as the queen of the dragons. When she brought them all together, do you think she knew what she had done?"

"She might have, as I said, but I doubt it. The note that was left for her, where did you find it?" Sunshine told her that it had been under the king, with the two crowns that they had worn. "I would say that she didn't know, nor does she have any idea what they have given her. And indirectly to young Chase. He will be…well, I hope he will be more receptive of it than Jason might have been before meeting his own mate. Otherwise, we might have a greater war on our hands than we have ever had."

She didn't think that Chase would be a problem, not with this or anything that had to do with his mate. But Kilian was as sure as she stood there, in her garden, that Emerald would be. She would be angry at a lot of things, but mostly at her dragon for putting her into such a position. Kilian was both looking forward to telling her and not. This wasn't going to be easy, she knew it.

15

Chapter 2

It had scared Jewel a bit when the queen of faeries called the meeting. She didn't care for being in the dark about things in the family, nor did she like not having any say in what happened to Emerald and Chase. They were her family, and she didn't want them to be harmed in any way. She was, however, glad to have them all under one roof, hers. But for as happy as she was to have them all together — they were such fun — she didn't want them to get upset with each other. That, she knew, was almost a given. They seemed to relish in having something to argue about.

They arrived en masse. Jewel had grown up as an only child. Her father had been her hero and her champion, but he'd been quiet, reserved. These men, they were far from that. Each of them loved with all that they had inside of them, and showed it in big ways. But when it came to their father, they were loving, gentle, and sweet. It made Jewel so happy to see how they treated him, even if he was cantankerous and crabby at times. They were good boys, as their dad was fond of saying.

When Emerald entered the room, it was as if it the air

17

chilled around them a little. Not because of her attitude, it's just that she was naturally cold. The snow was thick on the ground, but Jewel thought that it might be warmer out there. But almost as soon as she thought about getting some extra clothing to wear, the room warmed up…not by margins, but immediately. She looked at the warrior.

"You have only to ask me, mistress, and I will accommodate you. This is your home, after all." Jewel told her that she didn't think about it, and just to call her Jewel. "No, but you would have suffered unnecessarily, and that isn't good in your own home. I'm not a monster…well, not always."

"Thank you. I think." Emerald nodded and looked around the room. "I'm not sure about a lot of things about you. I mean, other than the few things that we've read about, your very existence seems to be a mystery."

"As it was supposed to be." The rest of the people in the room seemed to quiet, and were waiting on Emerald to finish. Instead of just fobbing them off, which she might well have done, Emerald spoke louder, so that they could all hear her. "Ice dragons were a rarity even when there were hundreds of them. They're not large, not like you'd think, but small until needed. They can hide in plain sight, which made them the best kind of warriors. It was up to me and my kind; we would bring out their beasts when war was to be fought."

"Are there any of them left? I know that you're the only female of your kind, but what about the dragons?" Jewel wasn't sure she was going to answer her. So when she went to the door that led out onto the frozen deck, everyone watched. When she opened the door and two small creatures flew in to sit on Emerald's shoulders, Jewel realized why no one would be able to see them. "Oh my. They're so beautiful. Aren't they?"

Since they were made of ice, a glassy sort of kind, the

room and the things in it seemed to be reflected back. Jewel had a feeling that when they were outside, or in battle mode, they would either look like a small spark in the tree, a bit of trash, or a bird. They could be hidden in plain sight simply because of what they were.

"They're very young yet, but older than any of you. These two are a pair; mates, I suppose they'd be called by you. But in their world, they're pairs. They'll have children like them that will hopefully live long enough to have children of their own. The same as most woodland creatures, they have to be careful of larger prey, as well as humans." When one of them flew to Chase, Jewel watched to see how he'd react. "He knows what you are to me. He won't harm any of you in any way, so long as you don't threaten me or him or my mate."

"Do they have names?" When Chase asked, he put out his hand and the female came to sit upon it. "They're very cold, aren't they? I mean, I suppose as an ice dragon, they would be, but I didn't expect them to be this frigid."

"No, they have no names that I know of. I can understand them, and once we have mated then you will as well. They can be called upon to help you — again, once we have mated — and they'll do as you want, going so far as to kill someone for you." He looked around the room, and Jewel had a feeling that she knew what he was thinking. "Yes, even your family. Though I don't think that you'd ever request them to do that. As for being cold, that is necessary to keep them alive. In the warmer months they spend a great deal of time, when not working, deep within the caves close by. It is where they breed as well."

"You're right, never would I want them to harm anyone of my family." The female flew to Jewel, then to the rest of the people in the room. Her stare, Jewel thought, was very thorough, perhaps even deep. And when she went back to Chase, sitting once again on his hand, Chase spoke again.

"Was she getting their scent?"

"No, she was seeing if they could be trusted." Chase asked what would have happened if they couldn't. "They found them to be trusting. For now, that's all you need to know."

Jewel shivered. She wasn't sure she wanted to know what they might have done. Even though her mind was pretty creative, the kind of things that these little creatures could do to someone that they didn't trust was something that she didn't want to think about. Ever.

"How big do they get? I'm assuming that they can be really large when you call upon them." Jason moved to sit next to his parents, and when he was seated, the female again moved to stare at him. Jewel wasn't sure what was going on when the little dragon moved to sit on Emerald's shoulder again. "What's she doing now?"

"She said that you are more than a vampire. That you have been touched by the queen of faeries. It is her request that you let her sample your blood, just to tell her what sort of magic she can expect from you." Jason looked at Jewel and she nodded. "It's not necessary. If you do not wish it, then she will understand."

"No, it's not that. I have my own mate, and I'd hate to do anything without asking her first. I'm making up for some bad beginnings, and I'm trying my best to watch myself from now on." Everyone laughed, and she smiled at Jason. He was getting much better about not ordering her around like she was a lost pup. "If it's all right with her and Chase, I don't mind at all."

"I don't have a problem with it. Not if you don't." He looked at Jewel when Chase gave his approval. "However, I'd like to ask why she cares what he is."

"She cares because if she is in need of something magical, then she will know if he can help her. Also, should he need her, for anything at all, she'd know to tell him he could do it or if she should enhance his magic. You're powerful, Jason, but she is much stronger." When Emerald looked at Chase, she continued. "You are more powerful than even your brothers all together. And as such, you can do much more. You will be able to command armies."

"Will there be a need for him to be able to do that?" Everyone looked at Emerald when Jewel asked the question. It was scary, to her, to think that they'd need an army of any size, much less be able to call on them. "I mean, we've had a pretty terrible run with the bad guys, I think. I, for one, would like to have nothing to do with raising an army."

"There is always a need for an army. Even when there is no need now. Should someone take control of your family, by kidnapping or any other means of harming them, wouldn't you like to have the best at your side? Instead of wondering how you can get them back?" Jewel said that she would. "Then it would be good to have someone that can command them. To bring them to you when you need them to do whatever you need to exact revenge, or any other type of war."

It frightened her, on so many levels that she wasn't sure that she was ready for this. The need for war? Exacting revenge on someone? And how calm Emerald was when she spoke of it. Looking around the room, Jewel could see that a lot of the family was thinking the same thing, wondering how she thought they could justify anything remotely like she was talking about.

The exchange of blood was quick and painless. In the end, Emerald did it as well. They would be able to find her, and Chase, quickly should the need arise. Jewel hoped it would never come to that, but she was glad for the extra protection.

~~~

Chase stood up when Kilian appeared in the room

with them. He, for one, was glad for the distraction and the interruption. It had gotten very heavy in the room, and he needed a moment to think about it. As soon as she asked if she could sit down, Chase had a feeling that the conversation was about to get even worse.

"We have found the king and queen of dragons." He sat down and waited, sure there was more to that statement than just the finding of them. To be honest, he was having a hard time, wondering about the little dragon that still sat on his shoulder and what it was there for. "There was a stone note left with them on how you'd brought them to the cave to perish, Emerald. As far as we can tell, your dragon wrote it and left it for someone to find. He placed it under the body of his father."

"I did as I was asked by them." Kilian grinned at Emerald, and when she came to sit next to Chase he took her hand into his. "They were dying, they told me, and wished to be together in their cave one more time. Their age and the wounds that they had gotten were too much, even for them. They asked me to take them there, a special place for them, to be safe from humans. So that's what I did."

"You did well. In the notes that he left for someone to find, he explained how you had been so kind to his parents in their final moments, asking the earth to never say where they were. And that you stayed with them until the very end of their life cycles. Even your own dragon loved you beyond reproach, and he took his own life so that you could move on in your life and be free of staying with him until you too died." Emerald looked embarrassed, and he thought that was a first for her. "You have been given a great gift by them."

"I don't want anything, then or now. I only did what they wanted of me, as is my job." Kilian stood, as did he and Emerald, but Emerald backed from her. "I don't need it.

Whatever it is, nor do I want it, my lady."

The door to the back of the deck opened and in flew thousands upon thousands of small creatures. Not only were there more ice dragons, but faeries and brownies as well. As they formed a circle around Emerald, a crown appeared in Kilian's hands.

"By decree of the king and queen of dragons, I hereby give you the role you were born to have. You have been named as the next in line by them, and are now the queen of them all." Emerald was still shaking her head as several of the ice dragons took the crown and placed it on her head. When she looked at Chase, he felt something weigh on his head as well, and reached up to touch it. "You are king now, Chase. As her mate, you have the same role as she does. You should brace yourself."

Chase felt it coming over him, slowly at first, then more until he was hurting, like he was being turned inside out in that moment. Even as he fell to his knees, he knew that whatever was coming his way was going to make him stronger. But for now, he hurt. In every part of his body. His beast rose up, snarling at him and at the pain, and all he could do was let it go, have his beast deal with the pain for himself. Then almost as soon as he thought he was going to die from it, his beast calmed, and he knew that it was finished.

"You okay, son?" He told his dad that he thought he was. "Well, I'm glad to hear that. You sure scared the bejeebees out of me. Come on now. Let's get you up off the floor before I have to join you there."

Chase wasn't sure what had happened other than he had gained more power, but as soon as he was seated on the couch, he looked around the room. It was then that he felt the power rush over him in a good way. He closed his eyes, then opened them again when what he was seeing became unbelievable.

His brothers were glowing. Not like they had a light shining on them, but there was…. It occurred to him then; he was seeing their auras. They were all blue, with some red and yellow. He tried to remember what the colors meant and felt the touch of someone entering his mind.

They are blue, my lord, because they are caring, loving, and love to help others. They are also sensitive and intuitive. The deep red means that they are grounded, active, and have strong will power. The yellow, which shouldn't surprise you, is easy-going. The male laughed. *If it would please you, my lord, you can call me Sliver. I am the smallest of my family, and my mother called me that to keep me in line. She would say Sliver, you are going to be broken if you do not listen. I did, and now I could be the helper to the king.*

Why is it that I can understand you? I thought it was only when Emerald and I were mated. He explained things to him. *So the crown, it comes with its own magic. I guess that makes sense. Can I only understand you when I wear it?*

Nah, all the time now. But you should know that you cannot remove the crown. It will become invisible to all that won't understand its meaning, but it will be there, for all the others to see, when you are among our kind. Any kind, I would guess, but as I don't know many more than just dragons, then I cannot say for certain. Chase thought that was all right. It would be out of sight for his brothers, who would no doubt make fun of him for wearing it. *From only this meeting, my lord, I think they will tease you for it even should they not see it.*

Chase laughed, and in doing so, the room turned to him and stared. He just waved them off as he sat there. He was enjoying his life, and thought that having a mate that was a warrior could have its advantages. He watched Emerald as she spoke to Kilian.

Emerald was beautiful. Not only beautiful, but she was sexy too. Tall, almost as tall as him, and she was slender, her

24

legs long and muscled. He had seen them that morning when she'd come out of the bathroom with a towel wrapped around her body. He wondered what delights she was keeping hidden, and had to smile at their conversation that had come up there.

"I'm not easy." He said that he didn't figure she was. "I enjoy sex a great deal, but I'm not going to just flop on the bed and wait for you to service me. I have my needs as well."

"Flop? No, there will be none of that in our bed. As for servicing you, that would be my priority. To have you screaming out my name as you release would be the best part of making love with you." She asked him if he meant *to* her, not *with* her. "No, when we make love—and I have no doubt that we will, and soon—we'll be doing it together. As a couple. Your needs become mine, and I want you to enjoy it even more than myself."

She had stared at him for so long that he had a feeling that she was looking for flaws. He wasn't positive, however, even when she spoke again, that she didn't find a few and found him lacking in some way. This time he was sure she was teasing him, but Chase didn't know her well then, or now, and he wanted to talk to her about it.

"Men are selfish when it comes to sex. I have a feeling that you will be as well, I think." He promised her that the only time he would be selfish was when he was teasing her. "I don't care to be teased. You will do it right or not at all."

That was when he'd pulled her into his arms. Roughly, he knew, but he needed to show her what he wanted, needed from her, even now. The kiss was meant to mark her, to assure her that he knew just what he was doing. But when she wrapped her arms around him, Chase wanted more. All of her. And to give himself to her as well.

But the meeting had been called, and he knew that if

25

they didn't show, there would be hell to pay. They might understand—his family would—but they needed answers, and Emerald was the only one that could give them.

She moved around the room now like she owned it. But he could see a side of her that she kept hidden from others. She was terrified of them…his family. Not in a sense that they were going to hurt her, but something more. Like she was afraid she was going to fail them. When that occurred to him, he sat up straighter and knocked Sliver off his perch on his shoulder.

"She needs us." Sliver told him that was right. "No, she doesn't need us to make her safe, but she needs us to approve of her. To let her know that she's wanted here. And not just for her magic and sword."

"You think?" He said he was sure of it. "Well, then, I think that would be up to you in making her feel better, don't you?"

"I might need your help in this." The little dragon bowed and said he was there for him. "All right. Can you get into my house? I mean, it's locked up pretty tightly against the weather and such."

"You leave it to me, my lord. I can do whatever you need." Chase told him every trick and every romantic thing he could think of. Then he stopped and looked at Emerald again. "You've changed your mind?"

"Yes. I have. I want you to go to where she's been living and bring her things to my house. Our house, I mean, to make it more her home than it is now. Whatever you think she needs to be there, I want you to find it for me." Sliver was nodding, his face full of the smile he had. "And what I really need for you to do for her is make sure that, at all costs, you tell me when I have screwed up or I need to do something for her. I want her happy. I want her to be the happiest being in the world."

"Tall order, sir, very tall indeed. But it will be my pleasure to do this. Not just for you, but for her as well. Yes, it will be our pleasure." Sliver paused. "Her house here in town, it's gone, along with a great many others since those men came for her. She blew it up, just so they'd not have any clues as to what she might be. I know she's rebuilding for the people that lived in the place with her, so they'll have homes nicer than before. But I have an idea where her life is, the things you were talking about, and I'll go there. This will be wonderful, sir. Very nice indeed."

When Sliver flew away, Chase thought about what he'd said. Our pleasure? Then he shrugged. Whatever it took, he was for it.

Chapter 3

Walking around the kitchen, Emerald marveled at the things in the large room. There was everything a person could use to cook a large meal, and not have to use the same piece of equipment twice. But the large vases of flowers made her happiest. Emerald's favorite stem was the orchid.

"I hope you don't mind, but I had Sliver bring your things here. He said that they had fun doing this for you." She nodded as she touched her fingers to the light blue of the flower. "I had no idea there were so many different colors of orchids, to tell the truth. He told me that it would be our pleasure to help me, but I had no idea that he would enlist the help of so many. But those…I think those flowers are the prettiest."

"Thank you. And yes, there are a great many colors. Millions, I would imagine. They're beautiful." Chase nodded and stayed back while she looked around. The dining room, he called it, wasn't finished; he was having a new floor put in, as well as windows that were stronger. "Did you know that the faeries could come in and finish this in a day? They'd enjoy doing it too. This time of year there isn't as much for

29

them to do until the flowers begin to bud."

"I'll have to talk to Kilian then. My family plants fields of flowers for them every spring to help them out. It has a nice benefit for us as well. My brother Elliot, he has a nice shop in town that he has plants and such in. I think a few of them help out my other brother, Sean, when he's cooking, they help out with the fresh vegetables too." Nodding, she looked out the large picture window that was in the dining room they'd entered, and which had a view of the snow-covered mountain behind the house. "Do you like this room? I wanted to put a fireplace in here, but Dad, he said it might take up too much room."

"You could open the doors to the deck area, if you had some doors put in. And bring the warmth in from there. Even put in a fire pit; I've seen them around homes. A lot of people use the outdoors like that as another room. I think that's what I'd do. Have a room out of doors completely devoted to me resting." He said he'd do that, and Emerald turned to him. "But I love this room. It's warm with love and friendship. You have your family here, don't you? I mean, even though you think the room too small."

"Yes. We meet once a week at one of the houses we have. Dad, he lives in a condo...he doesn't care much for yard work and such. I think at one time he did that...landscaping." She said she had as well. "Me too. I think we've done just about everything at some point."

"Yes, boredom; it's hard to overcome if you sit around thinking of how much longer you're going to be living." She moved out of the dining room and into the large hallway. From that point, she could see into the living room and the large fireplace there. "You've found the armor that I wore."

The pieces had been forged of stone. It was heavy to wear, but very strong. It could take a direct hit from a sword or a spear and not touch her skin. However, if she fell, it took too long for her to get upright, and the enemy would be upon her.

"Sliver said he'd forgotten about it. It took a few of them to bring it in. I think it's a wonderful piece of history." She touched it, remembering every nick and mar in it. Not that there were that many, but those there, they were forged in her memory. "You must have been a sight in this thing. Or the other armor that they found too. I especially like the one that is from the medieval times."

They were in the living room now. Her swords—and there were quite a few of them—were hung over the fireplace. This place of honor, out where they could be seen, was very touching to her. There were other things on the mantel too. A helmet that had taken a hard blow to her head. A single legging, the other long lost on the battle field. There was a group of knives, most of which had been hand forged by her.

The couch had a throw on it, made of the fur of an animal she'd felled. It was warm when she threw it over herself, and she had good memories, as well as bad ones, about its usage. Moving by it, she saw her boots, leather ones that had been made from bear skin, sitting next to a pair of homemade snow shoes. A spear that had beads hanging from the handle stood next to the fireplace. Touching those, she knew where each stone had come from, the person who had given it to her, and the reason why. She turned to Chase when the memories became too much for her.

"I don't understand why you've brought these to your home." He sat down on the long couch and asked her to have a seat. She moved to the chair across from him. "These things, they don't look like you. They're violent, and some of them have been used for wars."

"I want them here because they're a part of your life… along with mine. This home is ours now. The spear that you

31

see there is yours, but on the other side, mine is there as well. I hadn't thought of my swords to be hung with yours until I saw the ones there that belonged to you. I, too, have fought in many wars; some of them we won, most we did not. But they were fought with passion, and sometimes love." She nodded and told him the same for her. "I want this house to be a reflection of the two of us. But if you don't like it, or wish to have these things put away, then—"

"No, I love them here. Some of them, these things, I've not seen or thought of for a great many years. They, like yours, hold good memories as well as bad." He nodded and asked her if she wanted to see the rest of the house and the things that had been brought. "Not now. What I'd like to do is touch you, and have you touch me. The kiss you gave me this morn, it made me want more from you."

When she started to stand, he told her to please stay there. As he made his way to her on his hands and knees, he spoke of the things that he wanted to do to her. With her as well. Her body warmed for him, and when he touched his hands to her legs, she moaned.

"When you do that, all I can think about is stripping you down and touching you with my tongue. My teeth." Nodding, she begged him to do it. "I think I'd like to take my time with you, this first time. Have you soft as putty in my hands."

"I'm nearly there now." He laughed, but it wasn't a making fun of her type...more sexy and romantic. "I know nothing about sex with mates. I'm sure that it's different than just to fill a need."

"I should hope so too. The thought of taking you, just tossing you to the floor and having my way with you, sounds so wonderful, but there is more to this than that. I want to make you mine in the worst kind of way."

She nodded at him as he pulled her panties off. The skirt

she had on disappeared as well. Her lower half was naked, but she wasn't cold. On the contrary, she was burning up.

Using his teeth, he took the buttons off her blouse. She was weak with need for him by the time he had it and her bra off. Breathing hard, she cried out when he licked her nipple, just the tip, then blew his warm breath over her.

"You're very responsive. I think you're going to love this." The thought of begging him to hurry entered her mind, but she knew he'd not. Besides, she didn't think she had the ability to speak right now. When he leaned his head to her pussy after pulling her to the edge of her seat, she moaned again. "I want to taste you. When you come, I'm going to drink deeply of you, and bite you as well."

"Yes, please." Emerald was dizzy from panting so hard. His breath at her nether lips was warmer than she was. His hands rubbing her thighs, her calves, and ankles were making her tenser rather than not. As soon as his tongue touched her clit, suckling it into his mouth, Emerald screamed out her release and begged for more.

Emerald came so many times by his mouth and his hands that she was weak with it. Her body was soft and warm one moment from a release, and then tight as a drum when he brought her back to the brink of coming again. When she'd had more than she thought a woman could survive, she pulled his head up from her and he smiled.

"I need you." He nodded and was suddenly naked. Magic; she knew that he had a great deal of it, but this was perfect. "I'd like to taste you as you did me, Chase. Take you into my mouth and have you come that way."

"No, not this time. If you so much as touch me, I'm done. I hurt badly enough now that I think I might explode." She laughed freely, and her humor at his pain felt good. "You think this is funny, love? Well, let me tell you something. The next time we do this, I'm not going to allow you to come until you're in this much pain."

Laughing with him, she moved off the chair and to the floor where he was. As he sat back, his back at the couch, she crawled up his body and licked his neck, his mouth, and his throat again.

"Your hands are so rough that I think you have been using them as a stone. And your skin on your chest, it's hard and flawless." He told her that he helped at times with some construction crews, and that was why his hands were so hard. The lick to his thigh had him pull her up for a kiss. "You taste of me, Chase. I love that."

He kissed her again, deeper this time, his tongue battling with hers in their mouths. When he pulled her forward, not releasing her mouth, she moaned when she felt his cock at her pussy.

"Slide over me, Emerald, please. I want to watch you riding me." She did as he asked, and having him fill her so nicely had her coming again. "That's it, baby, ride me until you come for me. Then I'm going to bite you when you do. I need you."

Excitement raced over her body. As soon as she started to ride him, her body a part of his, she bared her neck to him. When he bit her, sinking his fangs deep into her throat, she knew that she'd come hard and was looking forward to it. But she also knew that she needed to taste him too, so that they'd be together forever.

As soon as her climax took her, screaming out her release with his name, his teeth sank into her flesh and she came again. This time she felt the connection, the bond between them. And when he gave her his wrist, Emerald bit down on it hard enough to feel the bone crack. But the coppery taste of his blood had her coming again. And then again.

It was too much for her body. Her heart stopped for several beats, as if she'd died to become his. But it mattered little to her if she never breathed again. In this moment, Emerald took him to her heart, where he would remain forever. She was his, he was hers.

Tiny pinpoints of lights were behind her eyelids. Her body seemed to have come alive. It was as if she had stuck herself, her entire being, into a live wire. That was it, she thought as she tightened again for him. Christ, he would kill her at this rate.

Emerald let the darkness swallow her up. There might have been a time when she could have fought it off before the third or fourth time she came, but it was too much, her body was spent. And she had fallen in love with her mate.

~~~

"Department of Homeland Security, Agent James Nash speaking." Jamie tried to find the file that he'd left on his desk last night before leaving for the day. A few seconds of quiet made him pause in his search. "Hello?"

"Damn it, Nash. Where the fuck is that girl? Have you any more information on her whereabouts than you did before?" Jamie straightened his tie and sat up in his chair. "Well? You've had twenty-three months and nothing. Maybe I need to find myself someone else to find her."

It was on the tip of his tongue to tell him to do it. To find someone else to find the woman. He would have, too, but for the fact that he was going to be a father soon, and the income was helping them make the nursery safe. Jamie counted to ten, then let out a long breath before speaking.

"I've located her in Ohio. She's still there as far as we can surmise." He hated his boss. Agent Harold Bates had probably been in the agency since it was formed, he thought. Maybe the building had been built around the nasty old man.

"She's been injured. One of my men shot her."

And that had pissed him off. Jamie had told them, several times before chasing her, that they were not to harm her. Not to shoot unless she shot at them first. The fucking ass had told him he'd been under orders from Bates to bring her in at all costs. That was why Jamie thought about finding her alone from now on. To talk, not kill or harm.

"Injured, but not in our hands. What good does it do for you to tell me that when you don't have her here and answering questions for me? And with the simple fact that she's been around for decades, hurting her means jack shit to me." Jamie wanted to just say fuck you and hang up on the man. "You still there, you moron? Christ, you are one of the worst agents that has ever come across my desk. It's a wonder that you ended up on my team. I usually recruit the best of the best. I bet you graduated at the end of the line, didn't you?"

When the line went dead, he sat there thinking about all the things he could have said to his boss. Fuck off. I'm working as hard as I can. Blow me. And his personal favorite, die, mother fucker. He supposed that the reason that he kept all these comments to himself was because he really liked his job. And contrary to Bate's belief, he did a good job. Not to mention, Jamie had graduated number one in his class, both at the academy as well as college and high school. Picking up the picture that had started this, he looked at the beautiful woman.

"Where are you?" He asked her that daily, sometimes more than once a day. But she, like with all the photos he had of her, never answered. This woman had more names than all of the criminals he'd put away. "Just how old are you? Are you immortal, as he thinks you are? Or are you just a very good copy of a woman in your past?"

That was the million-dollar question. And to his way of

thinking, the only thing she'd done wrong in all her life was to come across the desk of his boss. She'd allowed someone to not just take her picture, but had had it in the newspaper a long time ago, back when photography was new, and pictures were in black and white. The one that he had a copy of, one that he rarely looked at, was grainy and dark. The article had been about women's rights, or some other newsworthy thing.

With the new facial recognition, her face had popped up a lot over the last few years. To him, there wasn't any way that this was the same woman from the black and whites he had. But the recent pictures were not just of her, though some of them were close lookalikes, but he knew it was no way in hell the same woman.

Her name, the one he had on her file, was Emma Green. It was, he thought, his favorite name she had used. He might have changed his too, the way people kept chasing her. It would be hard to have any sort of life with Homeland after you. By now he was sure that she'd changed it again...she might be going by something similar, but would still be hard to find.

He knew that her last known address had been in Ohio. Jamie couldn't believe how she had not only slipped by them, but she had blown up the entire building she'd been living in as well. And not one person had been injured that had lived there. His cars had been, but nothing more than a few scratches. And all the evidence that they might have found in the place had gone up with it. Which, he supposed, was her point. To leave no traces. And she was really good at that as well.

The file that he had on her was thick with pictures and information on her daily habits, which weren't all that predictable. There was a list of people that she associated with, two or three at each place that she had lived. Fat lot of good it had done them to find the names. None of them would talk about her, nor would they tell them where she might have gone when she left them.

No barriers on language either. She spoke to whoever she needed to, and left them with enough goodwill that they never had much to say about her when asked. It was like she was a fart in the wind, as his mom used to say.

He looked at the picture again. There wasn't any way to tell if it was her or a relative that looked just like her. Also, and this was what confused him more than anything, what did it matter if it was her or not?

As far as he could tell, she'd never been arrested. Never had any kind of accident or even a ticket, as Green or any of the other names that she'd used over the last few months. She had jobs where she lived and paid her bills on time, what little she had. Since she'd told the people she associated with that she was basically on the run from someone, there were no hard feelings when she left in a hurry. But his boss had a burr up his ass about this woman, and he wanted her found. In fact, it was something that he'd been working on for the last two years, and nothing else.

When Jamie's cell phone rang, he smiled. "Hello, love." She giggled; his wife of ten years was the love of his life. "What did the doctor say about the baby? Everything all right?"

"Yes, you worrywart, everything is going well. He said that the baby is in the right position, and we are both doing very well." He leaned back in his seat, forever waiting on the *but* in his life. But she knew him better than anyone, and answered his unspoken question. "There is no but, Jamie. He said that we're doing very well. I promise you."

"You know that I worry. About you and her. She's our baby, and you're mine." Kristie giggled again. "Tonight, when I get home, we'll tackle that bed again. I swear, those instructions were meant for someone much smarter than I am. And once we get it together, if we do, then we'll figure out those layette sets. I've got a list now, so we can go shopping for it."

He hadn't had to look it up. The women in his office with children had told him what he really needed and didn't need. He had learned from them that there were things out there that the furniture companies made you believe you needed, and you really didn't. But he was armed with a list now, and he was glad for it.

"You nut ball. You'll get it together, and then we'll work on getting the dresser in there. It's been ready for months." He told her that he knew that, he was pacing himself. "You're avoiding it because you don't want to have to move it again. I had no idea the thing was so heavy when I bought it at that auction."

It was, he thought, the only piece of furniture that they owned. That and the baby bed. His mom, a saint she was not, had let them use the house and contents until he could find himself a real job, one that paid well. But they'd never own it. Jamie couldn't convince her that he did have a good job. And no matter what he did with the banking industry in town or even right outside of their area, his mom would sabotage it by telling anyone and everyone that if they gave him a loan, then she'd make their lives difficult. And most of the people in their little town knew her well enough to know that she would, too. So, they were stuck in the house until he did as she wanted, which was to quit the Bureau and find a job that she wanted him to have. And Jamie wasn't going to do that, not if he didn't have to.

As for the dresser for the baby's room, he'd hurt himself just getting it in the place. But he'd not told Kristie that. She'd do it herself if he even kidded about something like that.

Kristie was like a bear with her cubs when it came to him. As he told her about his day so far, he looked through the file he had. That was when he paused on the truck that was at a stop light. Another thing that he wasn't sure why he'd taken when they were looking for her. But the truck had sat there for a long time before it finally moved on.

After telling Kristie that he had to go, he stared at the picture. There was something about it that caught his attention, but he couldn't figure out what it was. Laying it aside, he started laying out the other items that he'd collected. Most of it was just junk; a receipt for a restaurant and what she'd had to eat, in detail, and how much she'd left behind. He had no idea why anyone would care that she didn't eat catsup on her fries but mayo, but he knew that about her.

"So much trouble for just a relative."

He glanced at the picture off and on throughout the rest of the afternoon. There was something there, but for now, it was too close to him, he thought. As he worked through his schedule, he glanced at it once more and saw it. Just like a blow to the head. She was in the back of the truck.

Picking it up, this time with a magnifying glass, he looked at it again. Yes, it was a person. Maybe not her, but he'd bet any kind of money that it was. Writing down the plate number, he started to call in his team and decided that he'd check this out himself. That way, if it was nothing more than a wrapped-up rug, he'd not embarrass himself any more with his boss.

Going home that night, armed with the information and file that he needed, he moved the dresser into the bedroom and started on the bed. It was easier to move, he thought, because he'd taken out a little of his anger that he had at Bates in shoving it down the hall to the nursery. About half way through getting the sucker done, Kristie came and put her hand on his shoulder. He looked up at her and she smiled.

"Want to tell me what's going on?" He asked her what she meant. "You've been muttering to yourself since you got home. First of all, there are the names that you've called your boss. He doesn't sound like anyone that I'd like, by the way. Then there is Emma. I might have taken offense when you kept saying another woman's name, but I don't believe you'd ever leave me. Not now."

"Never." He kissed her belly and asked her to have a seat. After telling her everything—she was his best partner in his job—he finished up the bed. "I don't know what the big deal is, honestly. She could be nothing more than just a woman that is as confused as I am about why we're chasing her. I mean, Bates has this obsession about her that borders on insane. And I have to tell you, Kristie, he's really stressing me out about this. Between him and my mom, there are days when I feel like I'm not going to live to see my kid grow up. Always calling me names and cutting my intelligence. I can't stand the man, to be honest."

"Don't say that, honey. I need you. You're all I have in this world. Please, just let me help you. Okay. What is it you know about her, other than the picture? I mean, does she have any kind of record?" Jamie told her none that he could find. "And Bates, he's been having you search for her since you've been working there? All two years."

"Yes, and he pointed that out to me today. Twenty-three months, and no progress. I think I've made some good progress, but he's mad because we've not found her and brought her in. Why is that, do you think? I mean, why this woman, and why him?" She shrugged and rubbed her belly. Kristie had been a good attorney, still was, but with having a few complications at work, mostly not getting enough rest, she was on medical leave for a while. "Are you all right? Do you need a nap?"

41

"No, I do not need a nap. You will if you ask me that again." He grinned at her. "Well, I like your idea about going to see her. Without the rest of the team there telling him of your every move. I might like to go too. That way, we can say we need to get away before the baby comes, and it is Saturday tomorrow."

Jamie wasn't so sure that was a good idea, but as far as Kristie was concerned, it was a done deal. So he made arrangements to go tomorrow, with his pretty wife. They'd be in Ohio before noon, and then see her. It sounded sort of fun, really. And he was suddenly looking forward to it.

Chapter 4

Emerald sat in the empty field and looked around. She knew that the princess of the woods had been moved here recently, and she wanted to speak to her. It wasn't urgent, but it might be important for them both. As soon as Spud came to sit upon the grass in front of her, she waited for him to speak first.

"You are the new mate to Lord Chase." She nodded to him and he bowed. "The lady is working on the other end of the woods, my lady. She asked that you come to see her there, if you can. If not, she wonders if she may visit you in the morning."

"I'll go see her now." He nodded and asked to sit upon her shoulder. "Yes, but you know that I am cold, correct?"

"I do, mistress." She walked in silence. He was hanging onto her ear as she made her way through the trees and grasses. "If I might ask, mistress, what is it you wish to speak to her about? If you don't mind."

"I don't mind, but I am in the area now, and I wish to not just make her aware of me, but also that there are more dragons, smaller ones, in her realm. I don't want her to come

43

upon them and be startled." He said that was a good idea. "Yes, and if she won't mind, we'll need to see about getting more food for them, as well as fruit. She has the help of the Crosby family, so I would like to help her with this project as well."

"The Crosbys, they've been more than helpful with that. I have so many wanting to come to our realm that I have to turn a few away daily. It's a good thing, I think, to have so many people wanting to come around. But we must, like humans, pace ourselves so as not to over populate our area." Emerald agreed with him. "You'll see new fruit trees here in a bit. More than I've seen in a long while, let me tell you. It does my heart good to see it. When she was moved here, with the help again of the good gentlemen, she asked for trees to be planted. Gave them a list of things that they could find for her, and you know what? They brought her everything on that list. Pairs of trees so that they might be fertilized by the other creatures here as well."

"They are very generous people. I've come to realize that as well." Just this morning, she'd been told that there was a council forming to help her with the other dragons. Not that they needed one—she'd been in charge of them for a long time now—but to make sure that there wasn't any gap in the systems for their livelihood. Also, cold storage had been provided for those just hatched and in need of shelter. "You and Fairaday, you're happy here too?"

"Oh yes, my lady. Had it not been for the warning about the place we'd been before, I don't know what we might have done. Lady Jewel, she gave us enough notice that we were able to move not just ourselves, but all the creatures that lived in the glen as well. She is in our hearts now, one of us, as are you." She knew that as queen it gave her special treatment, but today she was going to beg for help, and offer her own services to help everyone. "There she be, mistress, near the apple trees."

Beautiful, she thought when she first saw the woman. Her aura was bright with goodwill and happiness. Emerald had never met this particular wood nymph, but she had known a few that, even in a larger glen than this one, were never as happy as this one seemed to be.

"My lady." Fairaday bowed low and Emerald did the same to her. She hoped they'd be friends of a sort, and she would like to be able to call upon her should she need it. "What is it I might help you with? I'm sure that we can help each other."

"Yes, I think we can. There are a few dragons coming to be with me. Not overly much, about four dozen. They are small, as you know, until they are needed." Fairaday nodded as she sat on the ground. "I would like to propose that I have some of them work with you here. To clear some of the land that you might be able to use. As well as they can get rid of any rubbish that you wish to dispose of. They are more than willing to help. I must warn you, I have a few that I have had some troubles with. Should you have the same, it would be helpful to me if you were to let me know. They know the rules of the land, but I'm afraid that after all this time, they think they're better than us."

"I've had the same trouble at times. I don't want to tell you what to do, my lady, but the best way to rid one's self of that trouble is to end it. But as for your help, you wish for them to be able to roam here?" Emerald nodded and said that they would be repaid for any foods they ate. "They only eat a certain flower and bush, I'm to understand."

"Yes, it's called a moonstone flower, the bush, it's the same." Fairaday told her that none grew in this area. "Yes, I've been made aware of that too. My dragons, they have the seeds for you to use. And since it is for their own use, they'll care for the bushes as well. I'm not sure that you would enjoy such a flower…they're very bitter and rather large. But should your kind wish, they're there for you as well. They have properties in them that might benefit some of them when they are breeding."

"I will have to see. Thank you for the information, my lady." Fairaday was a beautiful being with a kind heart, and her magic shone around her like a halo. When she turned to look out over her forest, so did Emerald. "I have been here for only a short time, but there is little that needs my attention as it did in the city. I think that I like that. It is a big area, and I can tend to a great many more trees than I did before. With the help of your kind, I think we could expand things a little past what I was working on. Thank you for that."

"The Crosbys, they told me that you were here at your own request. You couldn't do better, my lady." Fairaday looked at her. "I promise you, should there be a need for the dragons in war or just a show of force, I will give you as much notice as I can. And I would ask that should you find some strangers on your land, that you do the same for me. There are men looking for me."

"I am aware of that. They do not know yet what you are, do they?" She said that they didn't. "There is a man and his breeding wife in town. They only just arrived today. She is large with child, but is happy. The man, he is very stressed. His footsteps are hard and mighty."

She wondered who it might be, but knew that it would be someone after her. The fact that he had a breeding woman might just be a ploy. She would have to look into it.

"Thank you." Princess Fairaday nodded and stood up. "If you should need anything from me, you have only to tell the earth. We have an understanding as well."

46

"Queen Kilian, she has told me that you are going to be very helpful to our realms. That we were to afford you everything that we have to help you keep the Crosbys safe. They are family to her." Emerald hadn't heard that, only that they had helped the queen long ago. "You need anything, my lady, you have only to whistle for Spud. He is connected to all things, and to me."

Making her way back to the house, she thought again about the man and his wife that were in town. It could be nothing more than a person on a vacation, but she thought not. Her way to find out was to confront the people, tell them to go away and to not return. Perhaps even to scare them a bit. But with a family, a large family like she had mated to now, she supposed that she would just wait on the stranger to come to her, if he would. But that didn't mean that she'd not keep a close eye on him. Emerald called for her companion for these thousands of years, Soto, her only dragon friend.

Sunshine had come to her just yesterday and asked to be her companion. She'd told her that she'd have to work with her own helper, Soto, and Sunshine had told her that she must ask the queen. While dragons and faeries did work well together, Soto was an ice dragon and Sunshine was a woodland faerie. Not a usual pairing for two such creatures, but if they could work it out, she would be glad for the extra help.

"My lady, I was coming to see you this day." She waited for Soto to tell her what he needed. "I have spoken around, and there is a man and his wife here asking about you. Not you directly, but a woman new to town. No one is talking; I didn't even have to do anything so that they'd not. I like that, I must say. Using magic to hide you from their thoughts, it can be exhausting."

"I would think that was the doings of the Crosbys. They're

very well received in this town. What else do you know?" He told her what he'd already heard from Fairaday. "You will keep me, as well as the queen and princess, informed if they get into trouble here. I mean, trouble with us. Lady Fairaday has said she will do the same for us."

"I will do that, my lady. If you do not mind me saying so, the man, he will not last very long because he is most stressed. I can feel his illness when I am near him. He tries very hard to hide it from his lady wife, but she too is stressed, and this is not good for the child." This too had been told to her, but Soto was even more concerned than Fairaday had been. "I am keeping a good eye on him. More than the woman for now. She is worried about her mate, but is having a good time as well. She is buying local items at the stores."

"What would you do, Soto, if you were me?" It was a question that she had put to him many times over the years. "I do not want to cause any trouble for the family, but I fear with this stranger being in town, that he is part of the people looking for me."

"I would ask your mate, my lady. He is a good man. I have yet to meet him, but I have heard that he has a good head on his shoulders for one so young. But as I have said, I have yet to meet him." There was a tone there, but she chose to ignore it for now. "Also, the dragons have arrived. They are being put to work in the valley not far from here. There is a great deal of scrub that needed cleaning. And after asking permission from the lady there, she has asked that we leave the smaller trees for her. And the seeds have been stored away for use come summer. With the fields cleared, we can begin planting as soon as the snow has melted."

"Good. Keep them working. And we have permission to plant what they eat as well. The princess may need them to clear some of her own area as well." He said that he'd see to it. "Soto, you don't need my permission to introduce yourself to my mate. He is accepting of a great many things, and you will be as welcome as myself."

"I do not like to presume anything, my lady." She had to hide a grin; he was always presuming that he knew more than her and that his ideas were the best. "But since you have been remiss in making sure that I am known, I will do so myself. To the rest of the family as well, if it would please you."

"Yes, it would please me greatly." He moved off her shoulder but didn't leave. "There is more? What do you need from me?"

"I have nothing more, but I would like to say that I have never seen you glowing so nicely. I think it is you having a mate, but I think you are also no longer worried. Well, not as much anyway." She told him that she was happy and still stressed, but had someone to talk to that was a part of her. "You think that I am not a part of you?"

"Not the same, no. You are my friend and have been for so very long. You know me too well. But Chase, he is new to me and my ways, and when I pace, he doesn't pester me with questions as you do." He said that he was helping. "Yes, well, his form of helping me is to let me pace. I think the two of you will get along nicely."

When he was gone, she reached out to Chase and let him know what had happened with the princess. Chase told her that he'd make sure to look for the little dragon, and that he was glad that she'd spoken to the queen as well. He told her that he was busy working with his brother, and making sure that he was getting the best agreement on his new purchases.

I would very much like to meet this friend of yours. When we talked about him last night, I had the feeling that he's a bit annoying too. Have you changed your mind on that? She laughed and told him no, and that he didn't know the half of it. *I will try to be* on my best behavior with him, and not murder him for being a pain in the ass. Also, I heard from Jason this morning, and he said that someone was clearing the land near the lake. Is that your doing?

Yes, the dragons have to keep busy. If not, they cause mischief, and dragons can cause all kinds of trouble with their play. Chase laughed when she did. I have one more stop to make today, then I think I will be done. After that, I'm going to head home and try to get some work done there too. It's been a long time since I've been able to work and get things accomplished so easily. She told him about the man in town.

Yes, I've seen him. He and his wife came into the restaurant when I was there with my dad this morning. He seems nice enough. His wife is having a wonderful time I've heard, too. Shopping and meeting and greeting people. I think I'd like them both if I wasn't worried about why they're here. He sighed heavily. I was hoping, just once, that we could have a stress-free time without people trying to kill someone or even to take them. But we'll be fine, I know it. And once we take care of Bates and whatever he throws at us, we'll be better for it, perhaps.

She hoped so as well. Detouring to go and see the man, she asked Chase if he'd meet her at the hotel when he could. Chase told her that he was done there and would gladly go with her. Nip it in the bus, as Soto was so fond of getting wrong. Emerald headed there instead of going home.

~~~

Jamie watched his wife nap. She was the most beautiful creature he'd ever seen. And now that she was round with their child, all he could do was marvel at how much prettier she'd gotten, even glowing at times. When he noticed the flashing light on his in-room phone, he stood up to answer it just as Kristie woke.

"Trouble?" He said that he didn't think so, and answered the phone as she worked to get out of the bed. Reaching out his hand to steady her, he listened with half an ear to the man speaking. The voice at the other end, the proprietor of the nice hotel, said they had visitors. "Is it Bates?"

"I don't know yet." Jamie repeated the question from Kristie as she made her way to the bathroom. "Who is this person, Mr. Hamilton? Anyone you know?"

"Oh yes, sir. We all know Lord Chase and his wife. They only wish a few minutes of your time." Jamie said he'd be down in a moment. "Very good, sir. They're in the dining room, having some tea and scones. If you'd enjoy some as well, I'll let the chef know. He's quite famous regarding this treat."

After hanging up, he told Kristie what was going on. "Do you think they know why you're here?" Shaking his head, he sat down again to pull on his boots. His chest was hurting again, for the first time since they'd arrived, and he rubbed it.

"I don't know how anyone would know. I mean, even if Bates wanted to contact them, he doesn't have a clue that we're here at all. Or at least I hope not. We turned off our phone locator and took a great many detours to get here. Even renting a car from Indiana and using your mom's card and name to get it. I think we've covered our tracks." He hoped so, anyway. The more he thought about what his boss was having him do, the more he hated his job. A job until recently, he had loved. But the stress, he knew, was making him sick with worry. Rubbing his chest again, he was embarrassed when Kristie saw him doing it. "I'll go down to see them, and you wait here."

"I most certainly will not. I want to meet them too. All I've heard since we got here was how the Crosby family was doing this, how they have saved the town over and over. And the unemployment rate and crime rate here is almost zero." He smiled at her as she went on. "The schools here are the most up to date, and highly sought-after students graduate from here. This is a place that I'd like to bring up our children."

"If I lose my job over this, we might have to." She said she was happy with that too. "I know you hate the job, honey, but it's good money, and we'll need that with the baby coming along. We might have a better chance at buying a house should we have to stay here, but you know as well as I do that my mom will not make it easy on us."

"No, she won't. And I know it's good money, Jamie, but you're never home, and when you are, you're never home with me. Bates is not going to give you any break on anything. And the fact that we had to do all this to take a simple trip, it makes me worry that you're over worked too." He told her he was, to the point where just to go into his job was too much. "See? You need a break from them. I don't know how we'll live, but we did it before you had that job, and I'm sure we will be just fine if you lose it."

She was right on that as well. But he'd gotten used to having a nice car from this decade. Going out to eat with his wife when he wanted. There were other perks as well, but lately it had been the other things that were weighing him down too much to enjoy even the simplest of pleasures. Like coming here.

They had turned off their location finder on their phones as soon as the decision was made to come here, even going so far as to take out the sim cards and batteries. They'd bought round trip tickets to Indiana, when they were going closer to Columbus than anywhere. And after getting themselves a car, they had also bought several burner phones to use instead of their own cells. He'd not even brought his computer, for fear that it would be a tracking device for Bates. And there were other things he'd done to hopefully ensure that they had no contact with his boss. Liking leaving things undone at home, such as not turning the answering machine on. The house being watched by neighbors who liked him and Kristie. All in an effort to do his job.

He'd not told anyone where he was going, or even that he was going anyplace in particular. Only saying to his boss, via email, that they had decided to get away, and that since he wasn't on call, he wasn't taking his phone, computer, or car. If Bates emailed back, and he more than likely had, Jamie had made sure that he didn't open his emails after his was sent out. It was, he thought, the best he could do to enjoy himself, and to hide as well.

When Kristie was ready to go down to the dining room, they made their way to the elevator. He didn't know what this might be about, but he had a feeling that the police had contacted the man about the questions he'd been asking around town. Jamie had no idea what this man would have to do with the search for the woman, but he hoped that this was going to give him all he needed to go back home and tell his boss that he'd been wrong about the woman. Or something like that.

They had started out just asking a few people, but when that hadn't been helpful, he'd gone to the local police and asked for help. The police had been nice, even looking the picture over for several seconds before simply asking him why he wanted to look for a woman when he had one all to himself. It had been a good question, one he would have asked himself. But he was no closer to finding out anything than he'd been before.

The police had been more help than the fine citizens. The entire town was protective of each other. They had nothing to say to anyone they deemed a stranger, he thought. All Jamie could think about was that saying that adults taught to children. Stranger danger. But to him it only fueled his interest in the town rather than making him turn away. He would love to, like his wife, to live in a town where everyone had your back.

The dining room was busy, and he waited in line to find the couple. Kristie said she could eat, and he decided to ask for a menu. They'd yet to eat in the place, enjoying the little diners about town that had a flare to them that one didn't get in bigger cities, but he had heard good things about this place, along with the service.

As they were being shown to the table, he kept glancing around, looking for someone he might know in the form of his job. But as soon as he looked where they were headed, he stopped in his tracks.

"Mr. Nash." He nodded at the man who had shaken his hand, but he couldn't take his eyes off the woman at the table. "Come on, have a seat and we'll talk. All right?"

"I...it's her." The man turned his face so that he could look at him. "You can't believe how long I've been looking for her."

"Sit down." He nearly sat on the floor, but the man half guided him, half carried him to the table. As soon as they were seated water was brought to them, but Jamie couldn't even think, much less drink anything. The man smiled at him and introduced the beautiful woman to him. "This is my wife, Emerald Crosby. Emerald, I think this is James and Kristina Nash, from Washington."

"Yes, we are. It looks as if my husband has lost his manners, along with his tongue." He looked at his wife, who was smiling at him. "You're being very rude, my dear. And here I thought you only had eyes for me."

He stared at the woman, and his first impression was that the pictures of her hadn't done her any justice whatsoever. And the more he looked at her, the more he realized that she could well be the woman in the older photo. If not, then she was her exact twin.

"You're the woman, from the picture." Emerald asked him what picture. He hadn't brought the file with him, but he knew the face like his own. "My boss, he's had me looking for you for nearly two years. I'm with Homeland Security. I never thought that I'd ever find you. I mean, you're not her, of course. How could you be? You're young and very beautiful. But you'd be old, very old by now if it was you."

"You are making no sense, just so you know." He nodded, then shook his head at her. "Calm down before you have a heart attack, Mr. Nash. You're not well, and I'm worried about you. You're very pale, and your heartrate is through the roof. Calm down or I'll do it for you."

Jamie started to feel lightheaded. His head was pounding, and sweat was running down his back like a river of stickiness. Just as he reached for his glass of water, he noticed that his hands were shaking too badly for him to pick the glass up. He looked at Kristie and she was out of focus.

"I don't know what's happening to me. I do feel sick." He did feel like his heart was racing, and he felt all clammy as well. Putting his hand over his heart, he could almost feel it pounding. When dizziness swamped him hard, someone pressed his head between his knees and told him to breathe. "It's not helping."

As soon as his head was let go, the sting of someone slapping him had him feeling better. Not great, but he could at least breathe now. He stared at the woman who had hit him, and instead of getting angry, he thanked her.

"You're not in good health." He nodded, then asked her how she knew. "Because I'm not as stupid as your boss thinks I am." He nodded again and looked at Chase when he laughed. "He thinks this is funny because you have it in your head that your boss is off his noodle."

"He is. He sent me on this.... How did you know that?" Before she could answer, if she even was, salads were set in front of him and Kristie and a bowl of soup in front of Emerald. Chase wasn't eating. "I'm sorry. My wife, she gets the oddest cravings at times. If you've already eaten, we can talk, then have our meal later."

"Mr. Nash, what are you doing here? I know for a fact that no one from your office knows you're here. You have cell phones that don't have anything to do with your job. There is no computer in your room or on your person. There is Wi-Fi here, yet you've never hooked into it. And as far as I can tell, you don't have a thing to do with the other people that showed up a couple of days ago. Why are you here, exactly?"

Jamie started to answer him, then realized just how much information the man had. "You've had me followed?" He said that there wasn't any reason for him to follow him. Everyone in town had been watching for him. "Yes, we've run into that as well. You live in a very loyal town, Mr. Crosby. But I do have a few questions that I'm sure you both can answer. Please?"

"Yes, you do have questions, I can see it. But for now, we'll have a nice lunch and talk about things that have nothing to do with your work, or the reason my wife looks like a photo you have that is several decades old. To be honest, I fear for your health right now."

Jamie started to rub his hand over his pounding chest again, but didn't want to worry his wife. Jamie blinked several times too, hoping that his vision would clear. Taking a deep breath was painful. Hell, even a small one was hurting him.

Questions were racing through his mind at a rapid rate. And with them, his heartrate was going up until he wanted to lie down, to close his eyes against the pounding pain. It was beating so hard that he could feel it thumping out of his chest. Before he could begin to tell them that he needed to lie down, he was lifted up from his seat and carried away. That was all he remembered, besides Kristie calling his name over and over before he passed out.

Chapter 5

"What the hell do you mean, he's just gone? I thought you had a detail on him." Harold hated incompetent men, and he hated men who didn't bow before him when they entered the room. Not that it was necessary, but it would have been nice if they treated him with as much respect as he deserved. "Where is he and that fat wife of his?"

"I believe that she's with child, sir." If he'd had a gun, Harold was pretty sure that he'd lose his job today. Simply killing the man wouldn't make him feel better, but the blood splatter might. "But as to where they might be, I'm not sure. His computer is still at his home. Their cell phones aren't traceable. I think he might have removed the batteries. We were able to trace them as far as Indiana. Upon further search, the place where they were staying, under false names, says that while they did check in, they've not seen them once since Saturday afternoon."

"And now it's Monday morning and still no word. You do know that he was supposed to report to work this morning, don't you? Just like the rest of you? Where is he, damn it? Out with some woman? Doubtful, but did you at least look for him?"

Just as he was ready to send out the troops to Indiana, his phone rang at his desk. He knew that whoever it was, they were looking to get their head blasted off by him, and he snarled out his name as soon as he picked it up.

"Mr. Bates? Harold Bates?" The woman's voice startled him, and it took him a moment to realize that he'd not answered her. "There's no one there. I swear, no one wants to talk to me."

"I'm here. Just here." He felt stupid in that moment, and hated the woman for making him feel that way. "What do you want? This is a business line, not some fluttery woman's call."

"I know well and good what line I've called, mister. My husband is in the hospital. Jamie...he had a heart attack and they've put him in the hospital. And then last night, they transferred him to a bigger hospital in Columbus, Ohio." He had no idea who Jamie was, nor why he should care when the woman continued. "My name is Kristie Nash. My husband, James Nash, works for you."

"I know that." He had to let out a breath slowly. Twice now she'd tried to make him look bad. "What was he doing when he had this supposed heart att—?"

"It's not a supposed heart attack, you moronic fuck. He nearly died. What is wrong with you? My husband had a heart attack at thirty-three years old, and would have missed his child being born had not someone known what to do immediately. He's stressed, the doctor said, and he needs to slow down." She was so mad that he could almost feel it through the phone. And for some reason, Harold loved it. "He's not going to be coming in for a while. Jamie is very ill, and he needs to rest up and change his way of life. You're far ruder than I thought you'd be, just so you know. But when he

60

has a change in things here, I may or may not call you. I would imagine that you're the cause of most of his stress level."

The phone was still singing its disconnect tune when he put it back on the cradle. She had certainly put him in his place, he thought with a little laugh. No one, not since he could remember, had had the balls to do that. Looking at the flunky in front of him, he wondered what he'd do if she'd snapped at him like she had Harold. Probably cry like a baby and run off with his tail between his legs.

"Nash is in the hospital." He asked what had happened. "Apparently he's had a heart attack, and has been transferred to a larger hospital in Columbus, Ohio. The shit weed might be out for a while. Not that he was making much in the way of progress on his job, but there you have it. That was his wife. Why women think they can just make a call like that is beyond me. I should have been notified by a doctor. Or Nash. Women can be so fidgety that they make me want to smack them."

"Should we send someone there to make sure that he's getting the best of care?" Harold started to ask him why they'd care, he wasn't working right now. "His poor wife. She must be under a lot of strain right now, what with her having a baby. I'll see about getting her something nice to make her smile."

"You do realize that women have been shitting out babies for centuries, and no one cared a fiddle what they were stressed about, don't you?" The man just stared at him, in awe, he'd bet. "No, I do not want you going there to make sure that he's getting the best of care. The fucker left here without telling anyone where he was going. He can damn well suffer. But you are going to go there and find out what information he might have for me on the case he's working on. The one that he's been working on for nearly two years

61

without any progress."

Nash had told him he was going away for the weekend, but not where. He'd also told him that he wasn't taking his phone or his computer. That had pissed Harold off enough that he'd wanted to hunt him down and shove the devices up his ass. Nash was on call when he told him he was. All the time, damn it. Until he brought that woman in, he was on call all the damned time. And now, his little wife was calling him off sick. This shit wasn't the way to get on his best side, if he even had one, Harold thought. Looking up, Harold realized that the man had left him.

"He'd better be doing what I told him. Heads will roll if he doesn't." Harold worked on a couple of things he'd been putting off. There was an order that had come down just last week stating that he needed to be more in line with the rest of the departments. He was to hire two women on his team. Like that was going to happen. Women were too useless for any department, much less his. And he wasn't going to be able to handle being held to a standard if he had to either.

After he was alone in his office, he pulled out the file that he'd been keeping for himself. If he was found with it, he knew that he'd be talked to again. And while he probably deserved it, to him it had been a complete waste of his time. He knew better than most what sorts of things this woman could do for the country.

The woman's pictures, about a dozen of them now, were his ticket to fame. She'd had someone help her to figure out how to beat death. Not to mention, how to look like she'd not aged a day since she'd turned twenty-five.

He wasn't sure yet, but he planned to find out how she'd done it. Then when he was finished with all the tests he could do on her, he was going to put her in a cell and keep her there for others to see his creation. He wasn't really into the rich and famous, but to have people coming to him, congratulating him on his find, would be the best thing ever.

"Well, not my creation, but she will be my find." He laid the pictures out in a neat row and looked at them. "Damn, but she's a fine-looking woman. Fuckable, that's what she is. Just plain fuckable."

It wasn't a word that he used often. He had seen some fine women in his time, but they had never appealed to him on a sexual level. Harold knew that he might be considered to be a homosexual, as he did occasionally indulge in a little male/male sex, but he wasn't. He was as normal as the next man. And he'd kill anyone that said differently.

Nor did it occur to him that she might have done this all on her own. She'd had help, for Christ's sake. She wasn't anything but a pretty woman, and everyone knew they were as dumb as rocks. He looked at the woman in each picture and couldn't believe that no one else had gotten it. That no one had noticed that she'd been hanging around this here good earth for longer than she should have been. And his bosses hadn't either. Nor had they cared when he'd brought them more evidence. The conversation he'd had with Agent Lindsey still burned him a little bit.

"Why do we care if some woman looks exactly like her relatives? And in the event you are going to answer that, we don't care. It's just a woman with good genes. Why are you even wasting tax payer's money on this?" He told his boss that it was the same woman, through all the years. "Impossible. There is no fountain of youth, no one never ages, and as far as I know, there isn't a pill you can take that will make you live forever, Bates. So, knowing this and my feelings on it, get your head out of your ass and do some real work. There are any number of bad guys out there that haven't been caught yet. That is what you're being paid to do."

Harold had gone back to his office and taken most of the seventeen men he had on the case off the woman and put them onto finding others…the top ten criminals in the country, as a matter of fact. And then, when pressure had come down on him again, he'd put his newest employee on it all alone. And put him in an office in the sub levels, to work someplace that he'd never be questioned. Fat lot of good it had done him when he'd found nothing more than that she was someplace in…. Harold looked at his notes.

"Ohio. The fucker went there to find the girl on his own." He stood up then sat down. What to do? He had to talk to Nash, and today if he could. But he knew less about where he was now than he had before his bitch of a wife had called him. Harold wondered if there had really been any kind of heart troubles, or if Nash was covering his ass. Standing again, his exit was interrupted by none other than his boss, Patrick Lindsey.

"I just got a call from the wife of one of your men. Agent James Nash, as a matter of fact. Also, his doctor called me. Did you actually tell her that you thought that he didn't actually have a heart attack, but was faking it?" Lindsey sat down with a note in his hand. In the other was a file. "Christ, Harold. The woman is six months pregnant, and you not only called her a liar, but you told her that her husband was as well. What the fuck is wrong with you lately? Please tell me that you aren't still working on that woman case. That's what this is all about? You're still going against company policy and looking for a woman you think is immortal?"

The pictures were still on his desk. Lindsey stood up and fingered the pictures before sitting back down. For a reason that he couldn't put his finger on, that frightened Bates more than being screamed at about her. The envelope was put on top of them, then the file was opened. He cut him off before he could read whatever was in the file.

"He is where she was last seen. Right there in the state with her. He went there to claim her. Nash is no sicker than I am. And he's going to take all the glory for this. You watch and see." Lindsey asked what he was talking about. "Nash. I'm telling you, that woman has done something to herself, I just know it, to make herself never die. And if you'd get your head out of your ass for one minute, you'd see I was right."

He knew the moment that the words spilled from his mouth that he'd made a major mistake. Not only that, but he'd managed to piss off Lindsey more than he had been before entering his office. Harold was trying to think of how to get himself out of this when Lindsey stood up.

"You've left me no choice in the matter, Harold. I've told you, several times now, to leave that case alone. And you've been written up...a man with as many years as you have in this department has been written up twice concerning this matter. I'm sorry, but I'm putting you on unpaid leave until we figure out what to do with you." Harold stood up...this wasn't a way to treat him. As he'd said, he had a great many years of service in. "You will be escorted out, and your badge has already been disabled. I'm sorry about this, but this is all on you."

"You can't do this to me, Lindsey. This is my life's work. I'm the best there is, and you know it. I've been here since before you were out of diapers." Lindsey said again how he'd left him no choice. "Of course I have. There is always room for choices. I made a mistake in telling Nash's wife that, I'll admit to that. I was stressed out as well. I've been on edge for some time now. Ask my men, they'll tell you. I've been snapping at everyone.

"Yes, and you seem to be snapping at a lot of people, Harold. Not just the people that work for you, but even people in your neighborhood. You actually told one of your men that babies are shit out all the time. You can't say that sort of thing to people. It's not right. Not to mention, it's against the law. You're leaving." No more than a second passed before the room was filled with agents. Not in suits as the men who worked for him were, but flak jackets and guns out in the open. "These men will escort you out. And so you know, I've sent men to your home as well. They're gathering up any information they can find there. No working, Harold. You're under unpaid administrative leave as of right now."

Harold was taken out. He thought about fighting them, but they were not only bigger than him, but also younger. In his day he might have been able to take them on, but at sixty-one, he didn't even try.

His badge to get him in and out of the building was removed from his jacket and his gun was taken, as well as his badge that stated that he was an agent. The wallet that carried it was older than the jackass that had taken it from him. They even had the nerve to take his keys, all of them, as he was informed that he no longer had a car to call his own. While he was offered a ride by the police to a hotel until they were done at his home, he was given cash to eat on as well as to buy any necessaries he might need at the hotel. The envelope had only two hundred-dollar bills in it. This wasn't right, it was no way to treat him. What he needed was his job and office back. Harold flipped the man off and turned away from them all.

This was bullshit. More than that, it wasn't fair. What had he really done wrong but said what was on his mind? As he did every day of his life. People were much too sensitive anymore.

As soon as he got to the hotel, he pulled out his credit card. After trying four times, the man asked if he had cash.

They'd pulled his credit cards as well? This was bordering on harassment, this was. As he paid for the room with his only cash, he stomped his way to the elevator and waited for it to come to him.

"Someone is going to pay for this shit. I am not to be treated like a subhuman. I'm a fucking agent, by God." He looked at the woman next to him, who huffed. "Like you've never heard anyone curse before. Grow up, bitch."

Harold entered the elevator and pushed the button to his floor. When the doors shut, he was alone in the little cubical and he loved it. Fuckers were going to regret this, just watch and see, he thought.

~~~

Jamie felt like he was waking from a thick soup. He had difficultly even making his eyes focus, not to mention making his tongue work. When he was able to make out the person in front of him, he still wasn't sure what had happened, or where he was.

"University Hospital, Coronary Care Unit." Jamie made his mouth work to ask why. "They're saying that you had a massive heart attack. But you're on the mend now and they expect a full recovery. And before you get concerned, your wife is with mine in the cafeteria having lunch. She was hard pressed to get to leave you."

Jamie felt slightly sick. But before he could move up more in the bed, the man was there helping him, telling him over and over to be careful of the needles in his arms, as well as the monitor on his chest.

"I know you. I'm sorry, but I can't place where I know you from." He told him who he was. "That's right. We were to have lunch today."

"That was five days ago, I'm afraid. Your boss has been called; your wife did it." He had a moment to worry when

67

Chase laughed. "She's all right, that wife of yours. Put your boss right in his place. Apparently he mentioned that you might well be faking this, and she told him off. Then she called his boss. I don't think that went over well either. However, not toward her this time, but Bates."

"I'm fired for sure." He didn't even feel badly about that. Not like he might have a few days ago. "What happened? I know you were there. And that I saw your wife too. I might have been a little rude to her. I'm sorry."

"Don't worry about it. It's going to be all right now. But before I answer anything else, I have a few questions of my own." Jamie nodded, feeling less sick by the minute, but still tired. "What do you know of the paranormal? Not just things you might have seen on television, but in general."

"I don't know what you mean. If you mean do I believe in ghosts, then no. I mean, they're not real. If you meant other creatures, such as werewolves or vampires, then I guess I'd have to say no to that as well. My boss has it in his head that they're real. Or that people can live forever. I don't believe that either, just so you know." Jamie gave a small laugh before continuing. "You don't believe in them, do you?"

"As a matter of fact, I'm one of them. The vampire, not the werewolf. Though I will tell you that I know quite a few of the others as well. A pack of them lives near our home." Jamie laughed again, and Chase smiled. He could see his fangs now, and was sure that he was supposed to. "Had I not been there, when you had your heart failure, you'd be dead. There wasn't any saving you by medical means, so I stepped in. So did my wife."

"No, no that's not right. You said it was a massive heart attack." Chase nodded and stood up. He was close enough now that not only could he see his fangs, but how long and sharp they were. "Is this a joke? I'm not finding it very funny,

I'm afraid. I have been under a great deal of stress. Mostly from my boss, Bates. But I don't believe in this sort of thing. Please, tell me that you're having fun at my expense."

"You have been under more stress than a man like you should be under. And over a job. But you're going to be fine now. And it's not a joke. I'm a real vampire. My father is, as well as my brothers. All of us are." Jamie let him adjust the wires that were on his chest when the beeping started to go faster. "You'll have to calm yourself, Jamie, or the nurses will come in and think I'm trying to harm you. I'm trying to make this easier on you, but you're not helping me."

"I don't understand what is going on here. Is this Harold's doing? Did he pay you to come here and get me going again? I am working on the case, but there isn't any way that the woman in the pictures is the same person." Chase sat back down but didn't speak. "What is going on? Really this time, don't tease me. Tell me what is going on with all this."

"I'm trying to tell you calmly and without upsetting you again what is going on, Jamie. You had heart failure and I gave you some of my blood—quite a bit of it, actually—to save your life. My wife, she gave a little of herself as well to keep your heart working without damage to it, nor your brain. You're alive because of the very beings that you don't believe in." Jamie nodded, then shook his head. "I can show you, if you'd like. Bite you again. But I don't think you'll like that any better than me telling you straight out."

"You're a vampire." Chase nodded. "And your brothers and dad are too. And your wife, what is she, a faerie or something?"

"Ice dragon. Not that she's a dragon, but she is the queen of ice dragons. I will admit to you, I had no idea they were still around until she showed up one day. She was injured and had to spend a few days in my freezer to heal." Jamie

69

was beginning to feel like he was on one of those rides that made you dizzy, and it wasn't stopping to let him off. "You're doing well so far, I think. I've taken the liberty of keeping the nurses out. But you're doing great. That could be because I'm calm. You're not really calm, but you're not freaking out either. Your wife took it much better than you did, by the way. She's a hoot. We told her, not showed her, what we are, and she acted like it was an everyday thing to her. Which, perhaps it might have been."

"She's pregnant and has gotten in the habit of saying whatever crosses her mind. I think its hormones, but I'm not sure. You're a vampire." Chase nodded again. "I'm feeling like I've been drugged or something, and that this is all a wild dream."

Chase stood up and pinched him, hard, on the arm. When he asked him what that was for, Chase sat back down and told him he was awake. Jamie laid his head back on the pillow and stared at the man.

"You're doing much better now, aren't you, honey?" He heard his wife's voice and realized that at some point he'd fallen sleep. Or, and he was set on believing this, he'd never woken at all and had been dreaming all along. "Jamie, are you all right?"

Something occurred to him when he thought about what he'd dreamed about. The sun had been shining. It wasn't now…it was dark out according to the window that he could see out of. But the man, Chase, had told him that his entire family was vampires.

"It was daylight. He was here, and it was daylight." Kristie laughed and told him that Chase had gone home, but he'd be back. "Don't you see? He was here, and the sun was out. He's not a vampire. Christ, he had me going there. Did you see his mistake too?"

70

"Jamie, he told me that you didn't believe him, but he really is a vampire. He's very old. And one day, when he and his family were out, a house caught fire and the queen of faeries was injured. The Crosbys, all men by the way, went into the burning house and saved as many as they could. They even brought out the dead for her. And in return, she gifted them with the ability to be in the sunlight." Kristie spoke like she truly believed what she was saying. "I've met them all, honey. Well, most of them. The faerie queen was busy, I guess, as were her helpers. You'll just love all the Crosbys too. And they've been so kind to me. Making sure I have enough to eat and am resting. I told Chase why we were here, and his wife...she is that woman you've been told to look for, by the way. And we're not going to turn her over to Harold. I promised them."

Too much information right now, but she was telling him what she thought he should know. But his mind seemed to be stuck on that one thing. That Chase was a vampire. And he knew, deep in his heart, that he was telling him the truth. He didn't want to believe it, but he knew it was going to be right.

"He's not really a vampire, is he, love?" She nodded at him and told him to calm down. "How can I calm down when you're talking crazy?"

"You will not use that tone with me, James Robert Nash. I'm your wife. When have I ever lied to you? Not once in all the time we've been together. Now that man, Chase, is a vampire. He saved your life and you will be nice to him, understand?" He nodded, sort of afraid of his wife in that moment. "Good. And as for Emerald—what a pretty name I think—anyway, she's promised to show me her dragons. Not all of them, but a couple. They're as real as you and I are. And they're very strong too, she told me. I've met Spud as well."

"A potato." She told him not to be obtuse. "Sorry. I just

71

thought, you know, spud was a potato."

"No, he is a watcher, for Princess Fairaday." He nodded, thinking that he really was dead, and this was his punishment for something he'd done. "You should see her, Jamie, she's so pretty. Not Spud, but the princess. A real princess lives in the woods with the other creatures. Can you believe it?"

"Yes, I'm sure she is. I need to take a nap now, honey. Can you tell the nurse I'd also like something for pain?" Kristie nodded and left him. "I'm out of my ever-loving mind."

Closing his eyes, he let the conversations roll over him. Everything was not right in his head. Jamie knew that if he was dead, he wasn't going to enjoy the afterlife much if he had to deal with this kind of talk. And if he was only dreaming, then he wasn't sure about waking up either. Also, he didn't want to eat whatever he'd had to give him such dreams as this again.

Jamie felt the drugs float over him. The nurse told him that he'd feel better in a few minutes, and he did. Dead, or whatever this was, did have its perks, he thought as he drifted off to la-la-land.

Chapter 6

Chase wasn't sure what he needed to get done today. He'd been working on a couple of projects for a job site that he'd been trying to get going. Then there were the two things that his dad and he were working on that he needed to get started. But all he'd been able to do was stare at the computer screen that had long since gone black. He looked up, happy for a distraction, when the new cook, Dustin Harper, came in with a tray.

"This is a sampling of the foods that the missus asked me to make. She didn't tell me what to make, but asked me to make a sampling of whatever I could cook. So I did this. I hope you like it." He looked at the small plates and felt his mouth water. "Miss Emerald, she has tasted them and said that she can't decide. That you had to make the decision. I wasn't sure what I could whip up, but it was sort of fun just cooking for a couple of people instead of hundreds."

"What is it we're making a choice for? I mean, this all looks good, but I'm thinking that I can only have one." Dustin laughed and told him that it was for the dinner party they were having with his family in a few days. "And we can't just

73

have this all?"

"You can. I would need more help though. Which means more money, sir." He nodded and waited for what the *but* was going to be. "I don't spend money, not unless you approve. If you say you don't want it and take it out of my own pocket, my empty pocket, then those people are going to be real upset with me. Not you, but me. I know I'm babbling, but I think this is either going to be the best legal job I've ever had or the shortest employment. Either way, I've had a good time today."

"We're not going to fire you for needing more money spent. Nor are you going to have to take any out of your pocket because.... Really, I don't know why you'd think we'd want you to do this all on your own. We have a large and usually hungry family. Dustin, hire anyone you wish." He hesitated just long enough for Chase to understand. "I know that you aren't really trusting of us, and that isn't what we want. You were hired because you had a good set of skills that we needed. The fact that you have a record doesn't mean anything to any of us, because as far as we're concerned, you've paid your dues for it."

"No one just wants to hire an ex-con simply because I know the difference between clotted milk and sour milk." Chase smiled at him. "You don't know the difference."

"I wasn't even aware there was such a thing as clotted milk." He was really; Chase had been around for a long time. And he'd heard of a great many things that this man would be surprised he knew. But he was putting him at ease, and if a fib would help, then he'd do it. "You were checked out, Dustin. And I was told that you know that we're not human, nor are the rest of the people you might encounter here. That being said, you must also be aware that we're way scarier than you are, and if you tried to hurt one of us, you'd be dead before

74

you were able to get the job done. Right?"

"Yes, sir. I know that." He rubbed his head; it was a habit that Chase had noticed the man had when he was nervous. "Why me? I mean, I know that there are any number of people out there that can cook as well as, if not better than, me. And you have to know that I'm not really good at anything but food that sticks to your ribs. Not the fancy stuff that people with money like."

"Okay, I can see that. But I want to tell you that whatever you fix that we don't have to is going to go over well. We're a big family. I have five brothers, a dad, and sister-in-law. Usually, as a vampire, we'd not bother with a cook, but we've been made special in that we can eat when we want or not. Comfort food, it's something that we all need, and a great deal of it. You were chosen because Emerald—and she's a good judge of character—said that not only were you trustworthy, but that you could be a good addition to our family." Dustin nodded. "Now, we're trusting you to do a good job. You can trust us in paying you a good wage, giving you a place to live, and keeping you out of trouble. Okay? So, you tell us who you want to hire and, as was done with you, a background check will be made for them as well. As I said, we want you to be happy to be here as much as we're happy that you're here."

Dustin nodded, then left, but he returned a few minutes later, taking the uneaten tray of food with him. Pausing at the doorway, he grinned at him. Chase couldn't help but grin back.

"I'll be cooking up some comfort food for you all come dinnertime. And pies. I make a good cherry and apple." Chase said he loved cherry pie. "That's good. Also, I have bread rising in the kitchen. It's what I do, knead some dough when I'm thinking about something. You see me making bread, then I'm thinking. All right?"

"Yes, and as much as I'd like to see bread every day, I don't want you to be thinking too many stress related things. That could kill you." Dustin laughed as he left the room. Chase said his name. "Welcome to the family, Dustin."

Opening up his computer again, he smiled. This wasn't so bad, he thought, having a house, staff, and a mate. Chase thought about all the things he'd done to Emerald last night, and nearly forgot what he was doing again. Burying his head in his work, Chase knew that if he got distracted again, no one would get paid that was on his payroll, and his family would miss out on a few opportunities that might be out there.

They didn't need the money. Over the decades, not only had they invested well, much thanks to him, but they had saved as much as they could. Even going as far as to go without things so that there was money in the bank.

When they'd first been turned into what they were after the fire, it had been difficult for them. Being out in the daylight had afforded them so much, but it had also made it so that humans were more aware of them. And that they were jobless and lived forever. It had cost them a great deal of money to move around all the time, get identifications as well as new lives. But they'd settled here, and were having a good life. Not that there weren't problems, but for the most part, they had done well for themselves.

So, when the money started to come in, very little at first, they each had given a great deal of thought to how long forever was. And they didn't want to be without anything ever again. It was the starting point for him, to find things that they could put their money into and have a good return on it. Thus, Chase had become the money man for the family, and it had served them all well. Each of them were billionaires several times over.

He was just inquiring about the two businesses they had in the downtown area when Emerald joined him. Chase had noticed that while she was brilliant, she was also a thinker. If she spoke about something she really had it figured out, but wanted someone to either verify it or to tell her where she'd missed something. Which wasn't all that often.

"We have a visitor." He leaned back in his seat, asking her who it was. "Mr. Harold Bates. He's in the hotel that Kristie and Jamie were staying in. Not that anyone is going to give him information, but he's asking around about Jamie, and me. I've had him investigated too. I figured that since he was here, we should know just what we're up against."

"He's Jamie's boss." She nodded and stood up to go to the window that looked over the back yard and pool house. "You think he's here to cause trouble, or just to find out if Jamie is really ill? Either one of those aren't going to be a problem, I think. We can easily kick his ass or bury him out back."

"We might have to before this is done, but I think he's here for both. I called in a favor this morning to find out what I could about what his job function is. Bates is no longer working for Homeland, or any other branch of that kind of service. He's been dismissed. Jamie is on medical leave as of yesterday, with full pay and benefits. He will also have to see a company doctor, but I don't foresee a problem coming from that either." That was news to Chase; he'd thought that Bates was a forever kind of worker. "He wasn't supposed to be looking into finding me. Bates had been told, several times as a matter of fact, to drop the case. It's why Jamie has been working on this all on his own from the basement of the building. He was there so no one would ask about it. Nor was Bates very nice to a few employees, much worse than he was to Kristie. Who I like, by the way."

"Me too. What have you done to ensure that they're

both safe?" She glared at him, then looked out the window again. "Emerald, what is it? This isn't just about Bates and his treatment of a few people, is it?"

"He's off his rocker. I mean, he's not just obsessed with finding me, but he thinks that I've somehow gotten with someone, a male someone, because I'm just too stupid to have done this without help. I talked to his boss today. He told me that he was sorry that I'd been dragged into this mess, and that he hoped that I'd let him know if Bates tried anything. Bates seems to think that a person can give him this formula that can make him younger. Why would he think that? And that as a female, I can't do things on my own? Because he's stupid, that's why." Chase was worried. Not for Emerald, she could take care of herself, but for the man. He was walking on dangerous ground if he thought she was stupid. "There are men here with him as well. Men that don't care who they hurt to get what they want."

"And what is it they want? You?" She nodded, but didn't look at him. "You're worried about them? Or is it something else?"

"Worried for the rest of you. Like I said, they don't care who they hurt to get me." He nodded, not so much worried as he was concerned why she was so upset with this. "You're known to them. What you are. How you can be killed. They're armed with silver and with stakes."

"They can't hurt us with those things." She turned and looked at him, and asked him why not. "The queen, as you know, she gave us a great deal of power when we saved her and her people. And some of the power is our inability to be killed by a stake in the heart or silver. It will hurt, I'm not saying that it won't, but it can't kill us as it would another vampire."

"Who else would know this?" He said that they didn't

78

share that sort of information with anyone but mates. "So the townspeople, they have no idea that their benefactors can't be killed. Do they know what you are?"

"Yes, for the most part. I mean, we've been here since the town was erected, so they'd have to realize something was off. But from the beginning, they were told so long as we're safe and not harmed, they won't be either. And we'd make sure that they had all they needed to be a very good community." She sat down now, and he could see her mind was working this through. "Honey, you're scaring me right now."

"The townspeople, they've known for a few days that you and I are mates. I wondered why they'd never said anything to any of these people coming around here." He told her that he'd never asked them to do that, but that they liked her. "Sure, I'm so loveable. But these men, there are five of them not counting Bates. What will happen to the people in town if they start hurting them to get what they want?"

"Then we step in and make them regret being born." She looked at him for several seconds, then nodded. He wasn't sure if she was saying she agreed with him or that she thought he was off his rocker too. But when she stood up and told him she was going hunting, he laughed. "Don't do anything I wouldn't. And if you have to, make sure that you can hide the bodies."

She was still laughing when she went out of the house. He thought about joining her, just to watch what she was doing, but he had to see Jamie again, and try to make the man understand what was going on.

~~~

Kristie watched her husband. He wasn't doing well, she knew it. His health was fine, but it was the information that he was getting that she thought he wasn't doing so well with. When she started to tell him, again, what had happened in the restaurant, he put up his hand to stop her.

"You know, this would go much easier if you would just listen to me and have an open mind about this." He said that he wasn't closed minded, but that she was delusional. "Did you just call me insane? I have to tell you something, James. I might be pregnant, but I can still whoop your butt."

"You're telling me, quite calmly, I might add, that a vampire opened his wrist up with his teeth, fed me his blood, and kept me from dying. Honey, I don't know who you've been talking to, or what you've been fed, but there are no such things as vampires." She growled at him. "Nor are there werewolves or anything else you might have thought of. It's just not right."

When she stood up to...well, she wasn't sure what she was going to do to him, Chase came into the room and winked at her. Kristie had a feeling that he'd heard her husband, and was glad that he was going to deal with him. This wasn't going to end well for her dear husband, she knew it, but she wasn't leaving him, in case he needed her. Or he needed a bash to the head.

"How are you today, Jamie? The doctor said that you're doing much better, and might be able to be released in a few more days." Jamie smiled at the man as he sat down, and told him he was feeling very good. He thought perhaps it wasn't as bad as he'd been made to believe. "It was worse than you were led to believe, actually. You were all but dead when I helped you. We've talked about this before, you and I, and I don't think you're any closer to believing me than you were then, are you?"

"I don't know what to believe, to be honest. Kristie has it in her head that you gave me your blood, that you're some kind of vampire." Chase told him he wasn't some kind of one. She started to object when Jamie looked at her. "I think she's having issues with me being in here, and has her mind stressed out."

"I'm not some kind of vampire, Jamie, but I am one. A very old and very powerful one. I know you find that hard to believe, but that's what I am…my entire family is." Jamie looked at her then back at Chase. "We've had this conversation before, as I said, but with you being about ready to come home, you will be around us more and need to be aware of us."

"I thought I had died." He said that he had, that without Chase's blood, he would have stayed dead. "I don't understand this. Are you saying that I'm going to be a vampire? No, no, this can't be right. I'm sorry, but I just don't understand how I'm a vampire, nor that you are."

"Would you like to be?" Jamie looked at her then shook his head. "I didn't think so. However, if you change your mind, I would gladly help you with that. Now, I want to talk to you about what is going on with your—"

"Wait, wait, wait. I don't understand this." Chase asked him what he needed to know. "This. All of this. Why are you both acting like this is real? I mean, I don't know what's going on here, but I don't care to be treated like this. Kristie, this has gone on long enough. I don't like being treated this way."

"I can show you." Kristie stood up, not sure what was going to happen when Chase touched his fingers to Jamie's forehead. "Just relax and I'll be right here. This is the reality of what happened."

Jamie cried out and she felt someone touch her. It was Emerald, who she'd not even known was in the room. And while Jamie seemed to be reliving the nightmare that she could never forget, Emerald held her hand. It was just the security that she needed. When Chase stepped back, Jamie looked at her. Disbelief or something akin to it was written all over his face. She felt tears roll down her cheeks as he came to the realization that she had been telling him the truth. They all had.

"Holy shit. Holy.... I was dead. I had a massive heart attack and I died. Why didn't someone...? Well, you did try and tell me. Holy shit, Kristie, I was dead." She nodded and reached for his hand. "I was dead, Kristie. Dead, and I drank vampire blood to be alive."

"I know, love. I know. But you're fine now. You just have to listen to the doctor and do what he tells you." Kristie held him in her arms. "I love you, Jamie. I love you so much. And now that you're here with us, forever, you're going to stop being so stressed out and take care that I don't have to go through all that again. You understand me?"

"Yes, I understand. And I'm not going to...I was dead and given another chance, and I'm not going to mess that up. Not again." She cried as he made promises that she was going to hold him to. "I love you, Kristie, my heart, with all my heart."

He was her life, and the thought of losing him again was making her weak in the knees. When something touched the back of her legs, she sat down in the chair and held Jamie tighter. They had been lucky, so very lucky that the Crosbys had been there with them.

"Are you ready to listen now?" Chase sat back down, as did Emerald. Kristie held onto Jamie as Emerald continued. "A man by the name of Harold Bates checked into the hotel where you were both staying. He has men with him. All of them are well armed and ready to do whatever he tells them to. However, Chase has spoken to one of them. It turns out that this man is a friend of the family, and he didn't realize that Chase was a part of what is going on. He said that he'd talk to Bates and see if he could change his mind. I don't think he will. But they're here because of me, and I'd very much like to make everyone as safe as I can."

"You're the woman in the pictures, aren't you? I mean, why not, everything else that I've ever believed has been shot to hell." Kristie told Jamie to be nice, they were helping them. "I'm dealing with this as best I can, honey. I think I can be a little snarky, don't you? Besides, I have a feeling that if she has been around as long as Bates thinks, this isn't the first time someone has been snarky to her. Am I right, Mrs. Crosby?"

"I'm sure that she has, but you don't have to take it out on a vampire, if you please." Jamie laughed, and she felt better about him. "Now, what about this conversation has me thinking that you're only telling us this so we don't get in your way?"

"Yes, I'm the person in the pictures that he has. And you're right. I think you've both suffered enough at this man's hands. But the issue isn't that bad, as no one believes him. You didn't even believe him, did you, Jamie?" He said that he didn't. "Neither does anyone that he works for. And you were only on the job because you were new, and didn't know that he'd been told not to look into the case any longer. Doing that and being a nasty sort to his employees is what got him into hot water, and now he's been fired. But that hasn't stopped him from coming here and trying to make a name for himself. And to be honest with you, I had only thought that he wanted to make this great discovery. Now it turns out that he's been made aware of what would happen to me should they capture me, and he doesn't care. I can't let that go unpunished."

"I had no idea that I wasn't to look into it. As you said, I was new, but now that I think on it, Bates had me meet him in strange places when I had information, and my office was so far removed from everyone else's that I never got to talk to anyone else. I guess he wanted to keep me in the dark a great deal." Emerald said that's what she'd heard too. "So, all this, have I lost my job as well?"

"No, and you won't either. I've convinced the higher ups that you were only doing as told." Jamie asked Chase if he wanted to know how he'd done that. "You might, but all I did was suggest that you were a good employee that has been put under too much stress to find this nonexistent woman. And that is why you had your minor heart attack...at least that's what they've been told about what happened to you. Also, there could be a lawsuit out of you having a heart attack when you did. Not against you, but Bates himself. I believe that is why he ran when he did. They're assuming that Bates sent you here and it was too much."

"Thank you. I don't...I've not been happy there since I started. And I've been working for Bates the entire time. He is a bastard, and it doesn't surprise me at all that he was handling others worse than he did me." Kristie looked at her husband when he glanced at her. "I kept working at this job because the benefits were good, and it was keeping a roof over our heads. With the baby coming, you can see why this was important to me." Kristie kissed her husband, not realizing until then how much he'd suffered for them.

"We understand that." Emerald stood up and started pacing the room. Kristie noticed that she did that when she was thinking. Chase continued as she walked the length of the room. "You're going to remain under sick leave for the next several months. The doctors here, friends of ours as well, have sent in all the necessary paperwork to keep you paid, as well as here where you have relatives. I'm your cousin, as far as they know."

Emerald stopped moving and spoke then. "Basically, we've decided that we want you both to remain here, well after this is all finished. Chase and I have talked it over, and we'd very much like for you to become a part of our family. Extended, yes, but we both like you and want you to be safe." Kristie said that she liked them as well. "Bates is in trouble with his firm. As in, just yesterday, he not only lost his job, but his pension, as well as a few other perks he was getting. While I don't care what he tries on us, I don't want anything to happen to the two of you. Nor the babe that you carry."

Kristie had seen a doctor just that morning. Emerald had set it up. Also, all their things had been moved to a nice little furnished house. It was close to the hospital so that she could walk if she wanted, but a car had been provided for her should she want it. Things were starting to click into place, and she'd just realized how wealthy and connected these people were.

"What are you?" Kristie was embarrassed as soon as the question came out of her mouth. "I'm sorry. I don't mean to be rude, but you're not a vampire, are you? And I don't think you're a shifter, or whatever they're called."

"I'm a protector and warrior. I am also the queen of the ice dragons." Kristie knew this, of course, but she'd yet to meet the creatures. They'd be very noticeable, she thought, if they were around. "Until they're called upon to war, they're small, no bigger than a pixie or a faerie."

"I see. And are there many of them?" Emerald put out her hand and a little lizard like thing appeared. Standing up, Kristie got closer and could see that it was indeed a dragon, and as brilliant as a diamond. And small. "May I hold him?"

"She. And if she allows it, yes." Kristie put out her hand and the little dragon flew to her palm. She was cold, which Kristie was sure was the point of her being an ice dragon, and when she spread out her wings and sat up, Kristie noticed that even as tiny as it was, it was very scary looking.

When she left her to land on Jamie, Kristie felt her baby kick and move. Rubbing her swollen belly, she thought of what Emerald had said. They got larger when there was a need. They were commanded by her. Looking at the woman again, Kristie took a step back. Emerald was dressed from head to toe in glass...no, not glass, but ice. Sitting down, she knew that no matter what Bates threw at them, they'd all come out all right. They had a warrior on their side.

Chapter 7

Harold didn't care for this little town. First of all, there wasn't a good place for him to get a cup of coffee. Oh sure, he could have some *coffee*, but it wasn't anything that he'd pour over his plants. Just plain old ground coffee without a hint of any other flavors, and the cream was just cow's milk. Disgusting. Not to mention, they actually served it in cups. Not the tall paper kind that he could carry around with him, but cups that were too small for him to enjoy. The place was so backwater that he wanted to scream at them to come to this century.

The second thing was, there wasn't any sort of night life. Not a single bar that was open that didn't just serve beer. He could have bottled, canned, or on tap, but no designer beers. Nor was there any way for him to order a relaxing drink. When he'd asked the girl at the little dive he'd eaten at for an old fashioned, she asked him old fashioned what, then went on to tell him that all their dinners were freshly made, and they even made their own pies.

He'd eaten fried chicken, not baked. White bread…no, there wasn't any other kind, he'd been told. Mashed potatoes that had been made with real potatoes, which he didn't understand the difference, and green beans with tiny bits of bacon in them. Harold concluded that they were all going to die of heart failure, and he'd be the only healthy person around when it was said and done.

That wasn't to say it wasn't good, because it was, but the way they slapped gravy on everything, slathered butter atop the bread like it was a condiment, and served tea so sweet that it hurt your teeth, he knew he'd be dead within a week of living here. No, he thought, the sooner he was out of here, the better health-wise he'd be.

As he walked around the place, looking for some sign of life, he found that it was much like that little town on television that Don Knotts had played the idiot in. Only Harold thought that the entire town was full of Knotts, and he was the only sane or educated person there. As he made his way into the hotel again, he saw the men that he'd hired and asked them to meet him in the room he'd rented. He told them to be there in thirty minutes. The man, he couldn't for the life of him remember his name, said that they wanted to speak to him as well. Good. The sooner that they were all on the same page, the better and quicker things would go for him.

Harold had asked about a room he could use, one with Internet service and a fax machine, as well as phones. Harold had been taken to a room about the size of a barn and was told that they could bring in phones, just to tell them how many, and the local drug store had a fax service. After inquiring about the phone numbers he'd use, they told him they'd all have to be the same one, as they only had one number for the place. And if he might need more than one line coming in, they'd have to ask the owner.

"Podunks." Harold went to the room in plenty of time to set up, then waited. He had had reprints made of the woman that he was looking for, as well as pictures of Nash and his wife. That woman of Nash's was going to tell him she was sorry for getting him fired. And Harold was going to make her call his boss back, tell him that she was sorry for causing trouble, and that it was because she was fat. Well, pregnant, which was basically the same damned thing.

The men came in all together. They were prompt, which he liked, but he thought they should be dressed a little more respectfully to his position. Shirts and ties and shoes. They were in T-shirts, jeans, and boots. He could also see that they were all armed, which he was glad for, but he couldn't help but be just a little nervous about it.

"This is the woman that we're looking for. I've heard that she might be here, but I can't get any of the people around here to give me any information on her. Also, I have an employee and his wife around this town as well. At least, this is where I've tracked them to." One of the men asked if they were getting paid triple for the work. "Triple? What are you talking about? There is no reason for you to think you should be getting triple for anything."

"We're here to find a woman, that one I'm guessing. There wasn't any mention of a wife and man. You want us to find them, then we will be getting triple the money you are to pay us." The rest of them just nodded, and Harold had a thought that they were mute, or they only spoke through one of them. Their leader, so to speak.

"No, you're thinking of this all wrong. These people, the man and his pregnant wife, are here, and I'm betting have some information on the first woman. See, I'm helping you, if anything. And you're to bring them to me so that I can question them." The man that had been doing all the talking since Harold had hired them stood up and said they were gone. "What do you mean, gone? What the hell are you talking about? You said you'd work for me."

"Yeah, we did. And now we're saying that we're not." The rest of the men left the room, leaving him and talker there. "You should have looked into things before you hired us, anyway. The man in that picture, with that woman you want us to find? He's a friend of mine. I don't hunt for friends."

"You're a fucking hit man. Your kind doesn't have friends. Much less people that they like. Mother fuck, what is this world coming to?" Talker threw the pictures back on the table and started away. "Where is my refund? When I hired you before I came to this place, I gave you quite a bit of money. Where is that now? I expect to have all of the money I fronted you, as well as the money for your hotel stay. My job is no longer paying me, and I have to keep all my money close to the vest, so to speak. So, hand it over. Now, as a matter of fact."

Talker laughed. "Yeah, you have fun trying to get that back. It's not like you can go to the police. What would you say to them? 'Hey, this guy stole money from me when he wouldn't kill or kidnap who I wanted him to. Can you please get it back for me?' Yeah, that'll go over well."

Left standing in the big room alone, he heard the distant sound of a phone ringing and had a sudden thought. They were using the hotel number in this room for him. But right now, it mattered little. He was without help. His men, they'd left him hanging.

Harold sat down and tried to think around the anger that felt like a part of his body. They weren't going to help him. And worse yet, he wasn't going to be able to use the money that he'd already paid them to hire someone else to do the job. What the hell was wrong with this world? No wonder they needed his department. This world was going to hell in a hand basket, as his old grannie used to say.

There was only so much money he could reasonably spend on this project. If he could get the woman to tell him how she'd lived for so long, he would be able to sell that information and make more money to pursue even his wildest dreams of owning an island. But therein laid the problem. He needed money to make money. And at the rate he was going, he was going to be able to watch as someone else took credit for his findings.

"And all because some upstart of a fat woman had to go and stick her nose into something that didn't concern her. Nash's wife, she's going to pay for this, I'm thinking. Even if I have to do it myself." He decided to go to the hospital and see Nash. "He might be able to have better luck with his wife than I would."

It had been easy to find out what hospital Nash was in. He'd called his secretary, hoping that she'd not found out about his firing, and was pissed when she told him she was glad he was gone and hoped he rotted in hell. He'd not done a damned thing to her, and this was how she repaid him? Then he'd decided to call all the hospitals in the Columbus area. He'd hit luck on the first one.

The trip to the big hospital was long and boring. He had no cell phone to use to email anyone, not that he had anyone he wanted to anyway. But with his privileges taken from him, it was impossible to hold anyone accountable for their actions. He could not wait to get his job back. And he would too. As soon as things started going his way.

The hospital was a nightmare. He just wanted to see one person, and that person seemed to have disappeared. Harold held his temper as well as he could, but he knew that a couple of times he'd lost it. Thus the reason he was sitting in the emergency room, waiting for someone, a manager, to come and talk to him. The security guard that was with him was not only armed, but he seemed to have an eye on him that made Harold feel like he was going to the chair.

"Mr. Bates?" He told the woman he was Agent Bates. "Not according to your old boss, you're not. He asks that we tell you to come home and forget this nonsense."

"I see. And is there, by chance, a person, a man that is your boss, I could talk to? I don't mean to be rude here, but you must have a man around that is in charge of things. Perhaps you're good at your job and all, but I need to talk to someone in authority." She asked him if he was serious. "Yes, very much so. We both know how you got your job. And if you could just send him down here to talk to me, I'm sure you can get back to your position under his desk in no time flat."

When she walked away from him, he sat back down. He knew she was going to go upstairs and help out her boss in looking presentable, and he'd be right back down. Of course she'd be pissy, but that wasn't his problem. Harold needed results, not emotional women that messed around in a man's world. No woman, as far as he could tell, had ever gotten anywhere in big corporations without blowing the boss under his desk. Or on it. Not that it mattered to him.

It was why he'd never had a woman in his offices. Not that he didn't enjoy a little sex once in a while, but he never let a woman rule his dick. He promoted on work ethics and morals. Things that women nowadays had none of. And he was sure that they never had, as far as he could see.

Harold felt the sting of something hit him in the forehead. Then he was not just being escorted out of the building, but being dragged across the floor by his legs, his hands cuffed behind his back and a knot on his forehead as big as his fist.

"What is the meaning of this?" The police cruiser, this time one from the state and not campus police, was right in front of the hospital. Turning to the officer, he asked him what was going on.

"Well, you mean other than harassing the president of the hospital? Or do you mean calling her a slut? Either way, we don't treat woman like that around here, Mr. Bates." He corrected him about being an agent. "You show me a good badge with your name on it and I'll get this cleared up. But from what I was just told, you aren't an agent any more than you're a nice guy. Now, *Mr.* Bates, get into the car here or I'll put you in. And trust me, with the day I've had, you don't want me to put you anywhere."

Harold got in, but he was no happier about it than the officer that helped him. The woman had called the cops? For what? Him being honest? Harold was going to get to the bottom of this shit if it was the last thing he did. And he was sick of being treated as if he were some kind of monster. He'd about had it with women and their *sensitive* ways about them. He thought the world, now that he thought on it, was way too sensitive about every little thing that happened to them that they didn't like.

Taken to the police station, he was immediately put into a cell. There were others in the cell with him, deviants for the most part, and he sat in the corner and ignored them all. Harold only wanted to see his employee. To enquire about what he'd been able to dig up on the woman in question. And now here he was, stuck in a cell waiting for someone to come and talk to him about what he was to do about getting out of here. Then it hit him…he'd have no representation now, as he'd been falsely fired.

It took him several tries to get someone to come and talk to him. Mostly it was because when he shouted for someone to come, the others in the cell did as well. Mostly obscenities, but they were louder than he was. When the officer showed up, he banged on the cell bars and told them all to shut up.

Harold reached out to grab him so that he'd not leave him before he had a word with him. There wasn't any way that he was going to be in with these people without someone explaining to him what it was he'd done.

The pain in his arm nearly had him throwing up. The baton had come down on his elbow like a bullet in his body. Harold was screaming now in great pain, while the officer stood over him until he calmed enough to speak. The anger coming from the man was almost palpable. Like he was wearing it like a suit of armor. Harold asked him what the hell that had been for.

"You do not reach for my gun." Harold tried explaining to him that he'd only been grabbing for his arm. "I don't care if you were grabbing for my dick, you don't touch me at all. Now, I'll see if I can find a doctor that will come see you about your fucking arm, but I'd not expect too much. You did piss off a lot of people when you called the president of the hospital a whore."

"I most certainly did not use those words when addressing how she was able to get herself into such a cushy job." Harold watched the man with the baton as he started to walk away. "Is there no one here that can help me? I'm in a great deal of pain."

He was left alone again. Even his cell mates moved to the other side of the cell away from him. Harold was getting highly sick of this stuff. He was somehow being targeted for what he was. A man on a mission.

"I'm going to have to start making notes, that's all." His arm was throbbing now, and he was sure that it was broken. "This is not the way to treat a man who is an FBI agent."

Time to make plans on how to get this fixed, he thought. How, he wasn't sure, but he had to plan. First and foremost, he needed to get that woman and prove to these people that he wasn't a fool. Somewhere along the line that had been overlooked. Harold was sure that they still thought of him as a fool, but that wasn't right either. He was an FBI agent, and people needed to remember that.

~~~

Chase woke crying out Emerald's name. As he came hard, his body bowed up from the bed, he grabbed her head and held her to him. Christ, her mouth was hot and wet, and he loved it. As he came down, no other way to describe how he was feeling, he pulled her up over him and held her.

"You're officially trying to kill me." She laughed, and Chase smiled. "I love you, my dear. And anytime you want to wake me up like that, you go right ahead. So long as you know, I can play that way as well."

"I should hope so." He rolled her to her back and moved to fill her. "Chase, I have to go work today."

"Yes, so do I, but you started this, and now I find that I can't leave you hanging. What sort of mate would I be if I did that?" Her moan only fueled his need to satisfy her. "Christ, love, you're so responsive. I love that in you."

He touched her everywhere he could reach. Running his fingers over her smooth skin. Touching the tight nub of her breast, which made his cock stretch and fill more. Everywhere he touched her, everyplace that he felt her need, she gave him more. More love, more need, and especially more of herself.

As her peak began to rise up, so did his own. There was never a time, he realized, that he hadn't loved her...even before she came into his life, Chase had loved only her. It seemed silly, he knew that, but he would never feel this way for another person forever.

The release for them both came at the same time. Not only did she cry out, but he cried as well. Love, it was grander than anything he'd ever felt, and he wanted her to know it.

Kissing her, holding her body to his, he lifted his head and looked down at her. His mate, his other half. Telling her that he loved her didn't seem enough in that moment, and Chase closed his eyes at the overwhelming need to say something. When he looked at her, he knew just what he wanted — no, what he needed — to ask her.

"Be my wife, Emerald. I want to tell the world that I have found not just love, but everything that goes with it. Happiness, joy, companionship, and so much more that I'm sure there are no names for." Chase looked at her then, his heart now and forever hers. "Marry me and be my wife."

"Yes, I'll marry you, Chase. I love you so very much." He held her, not knowing what else to say, his heart and mind focusing on one thing, that she was going to be his and that she loved him.

He must have fallen asleep again. Her side of the bed was cold where she'd been. Getting up, he took a second shower, almost hating the fact that he'd awakened alone. But he knew that today was important for her; she was going to go back to the plant with Jewel and his brother to figure out what they could do to make the place friendly.

Getting a late start, he was in the car on his way to a job site when his phone rang. Pulling over, he answered it on the second ring and talked to his buddy Mac. Mac was in town for a hit, for Bates. But Chase knew that instead of killing the people he'd been hired to kill, he turned them over to the Justice Department. In turn, they could be questioned, and if needed, relocated. That was what he did for a living. Being a hit man was only a front to help out with murderers bent on making a killing, both figuratively and literally, with insurance claims.

"Your buddy, Bates, he's bat shit crazy to find your mate." They both laughed. "He is also looking for Nash and his wife.

He has a very poor opinion of women, in the event you didn't know that. He's insulted the president of the hospital, along with a few of the nurses that work there. The security squad is a good one, and since they're campus, they have as much right to maim and kill as most cops do, so they're on the lookout for him. Also, and this is funny as fuck, the guy asked me for a refund on the money he paid us. He's off his fucking noodle, Chase."

"I do know that. Sort of pissed off Emerald too. He has it in his head that she's not smart enough to have come up with some formula to live forever. That's the reason that he's been chasing her. Nothing to do with dragons, as we thought, but just that her image showed up someplace long ago." Mac laughed. He too was an immortal, but not a vampire. He was a pack leader that had been around for a great many decades. "You should come by and meet her. Hell, the entire family would love to see you again."

"Not this trip, but the next one for sure. We'll be hanging out around here for a while, by the way. The men that came into town to confront the ex-agent asked us to do backup for them. They're sure that he's going to cause more trouble than just with your family." Chase told him to be careful. "We are. Oh, before I forget to tell you, there is a building in the lower east part of town that needs some people, like your family, to go in and get rid of the nest that's there. They're a bad bunch of vamps, and are going to hurt some people soon if they haven't already. I only heard about it because I happened to be at the pack meeting here, and they were warning them to stay close to home at night. You know as well as I that were blood is better than sex."

"I'll tell the family. And be careful. Crazy people do crazy things." After hanging up with Mac, he told his brother about the house. *Mac said that they're out to hurt someone. I'm betting*

97

that they're the new vamps that were talking at the last meeting we had.

You mean the group that kept telling us we needed to be more aggressive? I would bet that you're correct. Jason paused a little bit, but Chase wasn't worried. He'd take care of them. *I'd like for you to go with me, if you don't mind. And Emerald as well. Hell, we might as well have all of us there, just to show them that we don't care to be fucked with.*

We can do that. When would you like to do this? He pulled into the parking lot of the first building he was looking at today. *Emerald is at the plant today with your wife. So any time after they're finished, that would be all right with me.*

So the plan was set up and they were going to meet at the building they were hidden in around six. Chase glanced at the clock on his phone and figured that he had plenty of time to do everything on his list. But, like he'd had happen before, he also knew that something would come up somehow and mess up his entire day. Laughing, he got out of his car.

Chapter 8

Sometimes it just felt good to get out of the house for a bit. Franklin knew that he should be getting ready to confront those young vampires, but he needed a breather. Some time to himself. As he made his way through the dense woods, he paused when he heard something. Someone was coming his way.

Tensing for the person, he moved to stand close to a big tree. With the shadows drawn around him, he wasn't worried about anyone coming up on him. As he stood there, hearing the crashing sounds coming closer, he saw her as soon as she fell to the ground.

Franklin wasn't stupid enough to go to her. This was the sort of thing that he'd heard had been used to catch a vampire since before he'd been born. But when she stood up, he noticed some things about her. Terror was like a blanket around her, and she was bleeding.

When she was close enough for him to see the extent of her wounds, he heard more sounds and knew that she wasn't alone. But when the six men, all of them young vampires, came out of the woods behind her, he watched them carefully but contacted his family as well.

I think we might have a problem here. Jason asked him where he was. *In the woods behind my house. The vamps are here, and they're chasing a young woman through the woods. She's been beaten up pretty badly, and she's been bitten a few times too.*

We're on our way. Dad, don't confront them. If you do, they might hurt you. They're young and incredibly stupid. He said he could tell that. *If they harm you or her, they're as good as dead.*

You got that right. When the young woman started running again, they began to surround her. *I'm not going to be able to wait on you, son. They're going to kill her if I don't miss my bet.*

Franklin went to the woman as the men began to call to her, telling the human that she could trust them. As soon as he appeared by her, he knew immediately that these men had done this before. They had a system, their plan to kill her nearly flawless. Circling their prey, having one of them stand back, being the good guy of the group. And once the person went to them, having no other choice, he would take her first, holding her for the rest of them to drain. It might have worked this time, but he'd interceded on her part.

"Hello, boys. What are you doing to this woman?" They laughed and told him that he needed to move on. That she was theirs. "The problem is, boys, this is my land that you're hunting on, and I do believe you were made aware of that when you moved here. Plus, someone might have mentioned that we get along with the people in this town. We don't feed from them unless they are all right with it. This little lady does not look like she's all that keen on you having another taste of her. Now, as I said, you need to—"

"Listen up, old man. We decide what we do and when we do it. And we do not follow the old ways." The rest of them laughed when their leader looked around. "You go on back to your crypt and let us handle this woman our own way. She

100

likes, it, don't you, honey?"

"Please, don't leave me here with them. They've been hurting me for days now." He nodded and tried very hard to keep his own beast under control. "They're vampires. And they said that they were going to kill me."

"Don't you know what you're there with now, honey? He's the oldest vampire around these parts. He's probably thinking that he's going to chase us off and then have you all for himself." The woman looked at him, and he nodded when she asked him if he was a vampire. "See, I told you. Big bad asshole is going to get himself killed too. Right along with you. I'm thrilled to be able to help him too."

"Don't listen to him, my dear. Yes, I'm a vampire, but I'm not going to hurt you." She struggled to get away from him, but Franklin held her. Putting her to sleep seemed the best possible solution when he heard from Jason. They were there with him. Laying her on the ground at his feet after putting her into a deep sleep, he looked at the men.

Jason and Jewel appeared first, then the rest of his family. Chase was alone, but before he could ask him where his lovely mate was, she appeared beside him. Franklin let out a long breath and told them what the men had said to him.

"You called our dad an old man? Christ, kid, do you have any idea who you're talking to? Not only is he the father of the kiss leader in these parts, but he's not weak either. You're morons." Elliot laughed when the men did, saying that he was an old man too. "Yes, and you know, it's a real shame that you're not going to get as old as any of us are."

"You think you can hurt us? There are six of us, and we're much more powerful than we look. You are barking up the wrong tree, jackass." Elliot looked at Franklin and asked if he was all right. He told him he was pissed, but all right. "What do you care if he's all right or not? Christ, you guys need to be getting with the program here. We're much more superior to humans than anything in this world. We need to rule. Now, give us our dinner and be gone."

"Not necessarily." They all turned to Emerald, and she looked at him. "Franklin, pick up the woman, please. We need to make sure that she's not hurt any more than she is now. I can hear her heart beating slowly. It might have been too much on her, I'm afraid."

Picking the woman up, her scent hit him right between the eyes. Franklin thought that he was wrong and leaned into her throat and sniffed her more. Christ oh mighty, he was holding his mate. His second mate.

He wanted to put her down. To go back to what he'd been doing and just forget this whole thing. The men, they couldn't have her, but Franklin needed to think. To...well, he wasn't sure what he needed, but thinking seemed to be the best thing. But before he could get a thought in his head that made sense, the little dragons appeared behind the young vamps.

"As I was saying, you're not the big fish around here. None of us are." The leader of the group of young men laughed at Emerald. "You see, you've been fucking around with the wrong family here. I would tell you that you're going to regret coming to our town. Or that you should be nicer. But we all know that you're not going to abide by the laws of this realm, are you?"

"Fuck no." The other men shook their heads, and Franklin wanted to tell them to think about it. That the being that they were messing with right now was even older than him, not to mention more powerful than all of the rest of them together. "We're going to take over this little town. Make us a bunch of baby vamps and then take over the state. It's what we should have been doing all along. Not trying to fit in, but to rule them. They should be slaves to us. If nothing else, they should be food for all vampires until we say differently."

"Is that your final say in all this?" The leader looked at his men, and when they said yes, he told Emerald it was. "Well, if you'd give me the name of your makers, then we can proceed."

"Proceed with what, bitch? You think you can take us on? Well, I got news for you, we're younger and much better than you'll be any day of the week. We're going to kill you all." Emerald didn't say anything, but she did lift her hands up and over her head. When two little dragons came to her, Franklin took a step back with his burden. "You gonna hurt us with your little bugs? Ah, look at them, they're so cute. And as harmless as you are. I'm telling you, we're shaking in our boots right now."

The word, one that he had never heard before, made the dragons move as one. Had he not been looking directly at them, Franklin was sure that he would have missed it.

The change from small cute creatures to large dangerous monsters was immediate. Their skins changed from a silvery white to solid ice in the same instant. Scales made their appearance along their backs, and spikes replaced the softness of their hands and feet. Tails as long as the tallest trees around them whipped out and took out several bushes, a few trees, and snow. Franklin nearly moved back again when Emerald warned him to stand still.

"These men have violated the laws of their kind, threatened my family and humans that did nothing to them but to live. I, queen of the ice dragons, sentence them to death by ice." The leader snickered. It was forced, and he looked terrified. "Kill them."

Franklin knew for as long as he lived the image that was set before him would forever be one that kept him up at nights. That he'd see it in the darkness of the night, and be

103

both awed and horrified by what he had witnessed.

No one moved, not even to go home, except the monsters, this time shifting back to their original selves. But Franklin would never see them as cute and harmless again. They were just as they were meant to be…large, dangerous killers. Their bodies would mean death; their breath, as cold as anything he'd ever seen, would now mean something more to him. Franklin looked at the small creature as it landed on the woman in his arms.

"Don't harm her." He looked at Franklin, then back at the woman. "She's my mate. I'm not sure how that is to work, but she's mine."

The dragon licked his small paw then pressed it gently on her throat. He could see the mark there, small and nearly invisible to most other creatures, but Franklin knew that for whatever reason, this dragon had marked her as his own, and he wasn't entirely sure what it meant.

"Her passage will be safe." Franklin asked Emerald what she meant. "Her passage from human to vampire. They nearly changed her, but in a few more hours, she would have died because they would have drained her and not finished the task. Those men, they hurt her in ways that she would surely have perished from."

Left standing alone in the woods, he lifted the woman more in his arms and walked as far around the circle in the ground as he could. He would never come this way again. The woods, for all their beauty, had lost something to him this day.

~~~

Harold wasn't sure what the big deal was, but he wanted more than anything to go home. He wasn't going to forget what he was on a mission for, but he was going to have to regroup and figure out a better, safer way. As he sat in his cell awaiting his hearing, he thought of all the things he'd been told not to say to the judge, so he could get out on bail rather than a longer sentence.

The list included things like not mentioning that he was far smarter than him. It would go over badly since he wanted to get out of there. He wasn't to mention the woman, nor his plans to capture her and take her back to a lab to interrogate. This one bothered him, because to him it was lying, but he had agreed to the terms of the attorney that he'd been assigned when nothing was forthcoming from his old boss.

His cheap suit that had been purchased for this meeting was a little loose, and that bothered him too. Harold prided himself on looking smart in suits, and having an ill-fitting one made him feel less perfect. Actually, less at a great many things. But his things at the hotel were being held for non-payment of the bill. Like he'd been staying there instead of this cell he'd been in. To charge a man who'd not been there was robbery, but he wasn't to mention that either.

When his name was called to go into the van, he did so without speaking to the officers. He was sure that someone was playing tricks on him again, but he kept his opinion to himself. There wasn't any way that this jail only employed women. Not to mention, women of color. In his day these people knew their place, and it wasn't working with the whites. Harold knew that it was a way of thinking that would get him into trouble, but he didn't care right now. He knew the way things should be done.

The ride over to the courthouse wasn't all that long, but the people in the van with him smelled bad, and he wanted as far away from them as he could get. The aroma was almost more than he could stand, and when the van finally stopped, it was all he could do not to knock the ones in front of him down and make a dash for the door.

Sitting in the courtroom, he looked around. Christ, it was as bad as he'd ever seen in a small town. There were chalk boards on the walls as well as above them, with cursive letters like you'd find in a kid's class room. As they were all told to stand, Harold wanted to tell them that this wasn't even right, but the judge, Judge Merkle, spoke before he could. It was a damned woman again.

"I want to thank the elementary school for the use of this room today. The renovations, from what I've been told, are coming along nicely for the new courtrooms." She looked around the little room, then smiled. "I think I might have had second grade in here, a long time ago."

Everyone laughed, and Harold rolled his eyes. Christ. This was getting more and more podunk all the time. And he wanted them to get on with it. As soon as the room quieted again, the judge lifted up a list and called off the first name. It wasn't his. Harold stood up.

"Lady, if you'd not mind, I'd really like to get this done with. This joke or whatever it is has gone on long enough, don't you think?" Judge Merkle cocked a brow at him. "If you don't mind me asking, are you even the real judge? You see, I think there has been a mistake. I shouldn't be here or in jail at all. I've made a mistake in voicing my opinion out where people can hear me, and I'll atone for that. But this joke, I think it's gone on long enough. Just get down off of that place, miss, and bring out the judge, the real one. I have things to do today."

"The real judge? I'm afraid that I don't understand what you mean. I'm the real judge." Harold shook his head and told her she was a woman. "I'm well aware of my gender, sir, and I assure you, I'm a judge. Women can be them too, you know."

"Not if you want things done right, they're not. You

106

see, the county lock up, they think it's funny that I've been incarcerated, and now they have nothing but females around all the time. They're pretty to look at, you see, but we both know that women just are inferior to men. They sleep their way to their positions, and that makes for bad things all the way around, especially for men in my position." She asked him what his position was. "I'm so glad that you asked. I'm a man who gets things done. A man who doesn't go for jokes like this one. And someone that doesn't, nor have I ever, slept his way to the top. I got there by hard work and good work ethics. Women, all of them, they just don't have the same kind of work ethics as men, and never will."

"I see. And your name is Harold Bates, isn't it?" He nodded, thinking it was good that she'd been told his name. "I'm also to understand that the reason that you're here is that you insulted a doctor at the hospital, that you tried to disarm an officer — "

"I did not try and disarm him. All I was doing was grabbing for him to not turn his back on me. That's not polite when someone is talking to you. Then he had to go and hurt me. I have a deep thrombosis of my arm. That's a deep bruise, in case you didn't know that."

"I'm well aware of what that is, Mr. Bates." He thought about correcting her on his title, but she spoke again. "Mr. Bates, you're old fashioned, aren't you? And a man set in his ways. Back in the fifties, but set in them anyway." He wasn't sure what she was meaning, but didn't ask her. Instead, he was moved up to the front of the line to be judged. "I've been personally handed your file before I came out here today. It seems that you've been causing quite a ruckus around town as well. What do you have to say for yourself?"

"When will the real judge come in? I'd very much like to not have to repeat my story over and over." She told him that she was all he was going to get today. "I don't think that's very fair, do you? I'm sure that you've done some amazing things to get this far in this town, but I don't want some half-baked woman here trying to tell me what I'm to do. Or passing a sentence that is going to be all emotional, or some other craziness that only another woman can understand."

"Mr. Bates, I think you should learn to keep your opinions and your rules to yourself if you want to make it in this world. You are in my courtroom, and today, I have the greatest pleasure of telling you that you will be remanded over to a trial. I have seen enough today that I don't even need witnesses to come in and tell me what sort of man you are. You've shown yourself to be trouble."

He was being dragged out of the room as she yelled for the next case. "Now wait one minute here. This isn't right. You can't do this to me. I'm an agent of the United States." He was told, several times, to shut up. When he was sat on a bench, his legs and arm were shackled. Harold was sure that they meant to do both, but his arm was still in a sling from the other day. He looked at the officer that was standing over him. "This is the worst case of women's stupidity that I've ever had to witness."

"You keep saying that, mister, and someone is going to hit you hard enough to try and knock some sense into your thick skull." He only snorted at him. "Look, I don't know where you're from, don't really care, but you have to keep your mouth closed or they're going to tar and feather you."

"Yes, because that's the way things work. Let me guess, some woman figured that out as a punishment, right?" The officer only looked at him. "You can't seriously want to work with a woman, do you? In my day, women were treated the way they acted. If you were bad, then a slap or two was all right. Now days, a woman can beat up a man just as easily as a man can, and not even suffer any kind of jail time. I swear to you, women are the ruination of the world."

Harold looked around and saw his employee. When he started to rise up to go to him, he nearly fell on his face. Yelling for Nash to come to him, he was dismayed to see that he was hobbling around with a cane. The woman next to him, he figured it was his fat wife, was telling him to come home now and not bother with him.

"He works for me. You go on over there and knit something." She stiffened, and he laughed. "Look, lady, I don't care if you are fat with a brat or just don't know when to push your chair away from the table soon enough. Go away until us men are done talking."

He should have seen it coming. Christ, the entire town was against him. But almost as soon as the words left his mouth, he was hit, twice. And when he was going down, his only thought was, he needed to get home before he had to really hurt someone. Or someone killed him.

Chapter 9

Chase caught himself staring off into space again. He'd been doing that off and on since his dad had taken Brandy Snow up to the spare bedroom over an hour ago. He looked up when someone came into the room, and smiled at Emerald.

"You should know that your dad is in a strange mood. I think he thought that we were playing with him. Once I explained to him that we weren't, we had no idea, he's been in this strange mood since." He asked what he was doing. "Just staring at her. I've made sure that she's comfortable and not too sick. She might have been had the dragons not intervened. Also, I think he's a little freaked out about me too because of the way those men died."

"If you want to know the truth, so am I. A little anyway. Not of you, but the way they were killed by the dragons." She asked why. "I guess.... You know, I have no idea why I thought they'd just die when the ice hit them. I mean, they did, but.... Let me start over. I never saw anyone die that way before. And as long as I live, I don't want to ever again."

Emerald sat down on the chair and didn't say anything. Chase wasn't sure she was in any less of a strange mood either, not after the death of those vampires. And he was sure that he'd hurt her feelings too. Chase hadn't meant to, but he was going to be honest with her about everything. When she sat there, he thought about the vampires and the dragons.

When Emerald had said for them to kill them, he could see that the young vampires had thought, somehow, that it had been a joke. But when the dragons had reared back on their hind legs and drawn in air, he'd watched the vampire leader to see if he would run. Chase wasn't sure what the dragons would have done had he run, but since he didn't, the breath hit him first.

They were encased in ice in seconds. Not just encased, but he could see that it had filled their lungs too. Their bloodstream was stopped because of the cold...he knew this because he could feel it. The dragons, he knew then, were as much a part of him as they were Emerald. The vampire's eyes were opened wide in shock, and Chase could see the man's tongue as it had been helping him to form a word. A word that none of them would ever hear.

As the breath stopped blowing over them, the dragons turned their backs on the vampires. The three of them, each larger than a full-sized SUV, had swung their tails around quickly, knocking the frozen vampires over and shattering them into millions of pieces. There wasn't even a piece of them left that was much larger than the dragons when they were small. They had shattered any chance of them every coming back from—

"Chase?" Dragging himself from his memories, he looked at Emerald when she said his name a second time. "Are you upset with me?"

"Upset? Why would you think that?" She said because she'd killed the men. "No, not upset about that at all. I don't think that any of us are upset about that. I think that the dragons, that sort of scared us a little. They were so quick, so deadly, that I think that is what is preying on our minds. I know it is mine."

"They would have died anyway, correct? Why not make it quick and mostly painless?" He nodded and asked her to come sit with him. "I'd rather talk to you. If I get too close to you, then you'll touch me, and I'll be lost again."

"I love you." She told him that she loved him as well. "Then why can't I hold you? Let you know how much you mean to me?"

"You want to distract me again." He laughed, and she finally smiled at him. "I don't want to have your family at odds with me. I have come to love them very much, and when they look at me now, it's as if they're afraid of me. I don't care for that."

"Neither do I, and I'm sorry for that." She nodded and leaned back on the chair. "How about we have them over for dinner tonight? That way, if they have questions they can ask them, and you can answer them. I'm sure they do. I have a couple of my own."

"Dustin is making dinner tonight in anticipation of them coming over." Chase got up and went to her, asking her what they were having. "Fried chicken and potatoes. I'm not sure what else, but he's making bread for sure. I tried to get him to tell me what is wrong, but he said he has to work it out."

"I think I might be able to help you with that. A man by the name of Bowery—I don't know if that's a last name or first—but he called here to find out if Dustin is ready to go on a couple of runs with him." She asked what he'd told him. "Dustin told him no, but the man is making trouble for him, and a couple of the others working here. The gardener is a friend of Dustin's as well."

"Yes, so is the guy who is going to take care of the trees.

Just the fruit ones. Apparently he's also going to work with Fairaday." Chase had heard that as well. "What sort of runs is he talking about, and what sort of trouble is he making?"

"He's thinking on it, and so you know, he has no intentions of going anywhere that will get him into prison again. But I think he's thinking of a way to make it stop. I've told him to talk to the local pack. They'd watch out for them coming around." Emerald nodded. "I wanted to talk to you about Jamie and his wife. She said that she needs something to do. I don't know what she's capable of doing, but I would say pretty much anything she wants. And she has a law degree too."

"I was thinking on that. There are some classes that she can take that will bring her up on pack law. And there are any number of paranormal laws that she could learn as well. She could be the attorney for the family, as well as the pack and kiss." Chase liked that idea. "Jamie is going to be a stay at home dad, did you know that?"

"Yes, he told me that he wants to be calm for a little while. I guess he's been thinking about it for a long time." Emerald moved to lean her head on his shoulder, and he adjusted her so that she was leaning on his chest. "Bates is in the hospital. He tried to talk to Jamie when he was in the courthouse today. His boss wanted to meet with him and his doctor to figure out a long-term plan for him and his family. There was some confusion about where he was supposed to go, and Jamie and Kristie ended up at the hearing for Bates instead of the actual courthouse. Anyway, Bates said some mean things to Kristie, and then tried to grab her. Jamie hit him with his cane a couple of times and Bates went down. I wish I could have seen that."

"That man needs to have a good talking to. And I think that his boss is in town now as well, to not just talk to Jamie, but Bates as well. Something about unauthorized charges that came up on his card. There are some that think the man is insane, but I think it's more than that. I think he has real issues with women." Chase asked her what she meant. "He has it in his head that women should be home, pregnant, and waiting on their mates hand and foot. Something old school. He had words with the judge on his case about it too."

"Yes, I heard from Lynn just a little while ago." They both looked up when his dad and Miss Snow entered the room. Emerald sat up and Chase stood. She was nervous, he could tell, but no more so than his dad was. "Hello. Are you feeling any better?"

"I've been talking to your dad." Dad led her over to the other couch and she sat down, but neither of them looked to be very comfortable. "Those men, they're dead, he told me. That they attacked your family. I'm sorry about that, but I'm so glad that you all were there. I don't know.... Well, I do know what would have happened. I would be dead had you all not been there for me."

She started to cry, and Chase had a feeling she had been for some time now. As his dad tried to comfort her, he looked over at him and he could see the panic in his eyes. Dad was out of his element with a woman, and while it was funny, it was sad too. Chase knew his dad would come around, but it would take some time for them both.

"It's all right. We're all fine. None of us were even close to being harmed by them." Chase glanced at his dad when he didn't speak. "What else have you been talking about? Dad is quite the talker when he wants to be. I'm sure he's told you a couple of things you might have a question about."

"He told me that I'm his mate. I know what that means, but he's a vampire." Dad cleared his throat but still didn't speak. "He said that he's not like those other men, and would rather die than to harm me."

115

"That's true." She didn't say anything, so Chase continued. "Where are you from, if I can ask? I mean, I don't think I've seen you around here before. And I'm sure you might have family that might wonder where you are."

"I'm not from here. I've been traveling around the country for a few months now. My parents are gone, and I needed to get away." She looked at his dad, then back at him and Emerald as she spoke again. "They were very controlling, my parents, and I like being able to get out and about on my own. Then about three days ago, someone just appeared in my camper and knocked me out. I was hurt by those men. They bit into me all the time. I wanted to die. I thought that they were going to kill me."

"I'm sorry about that. I truly am. They're not going to be able to hurt you anymore...no one will again. As part of our family, we'll all protect you like our own." She nodded and looked around again. "Did you have any other family that we can call? Someone that needs to know that you're all right?"

"No. I don't have anyone left." She stood up and walked around the room. Dad sat down, and Chase thought he looked exhausted. "I don't know what's going on. As I said, I know what a mate is, but Franklin tells me that he had a mate before. Your mother. I thought, I'm sure that everyone does, that you only get one mate. But he's sure that I'm his. I don't want to be here if he figures out that I'm not what he thinks."

"I understand. Yes, but my mom has been gone a very long time." She nodded as she touched her fingers to the armor that stood against the wall. "You're his mate. Of that you can rest assured. As for it happening only once, that is usually true. But sometimes the fates have a different idea in mind, and that's the way it works, I guess. What is it we can help you understand?"

"I don't know." She looked at his dad, and he could see

that Dad was more confused than she was. "He's a nice man and he did save my life, but there are things going on that I don't...it's like I've been awakened from a bad dream, and I can't tell if I'm still asleep or this is my reality."

"You know that it's all real." Chase wanted to tell Emerald to go slower, but she stood up and went to the woman. "You also know that we can't, nor would we, lie to you. You're just afraid to believe your luck now."

"Yes, that's it. I can't be this lucky. No one can, but especially me. I've had it rough all my life...terrible, as a matter of fact, and now not only am I safe, but I have someone that will love me, and I'm not sure what to do." Emerald told her that she was and did. "But from what I know, they love forever, vampires do. But I don't have forever. I only have a few years, comparatively speaking."

"You have forever." When she shook her head, his dad stood up and nodded to her. "Yes, you do. As do the rest of us. We're immortal. The same as you are now. I meant to tell you. I should have, but I'm not...I don't have my head on straight just yet. But I'm getting there though. A man like me, he doesn't usually get two chances at love. I'm powerfully glad that you're mine."

"And you're part vampire." Brandy shook her head at him, but this time his dad pulled her into his arms and held her. Chase continued. "Yes. Those men, they did that to you. I don't know if their plan was to kill you or what, but they changed you enough that you are part of what we are."

"But that little dragon, he did something to me, didn't he?" Dad nodded at her and kissed the little mark. "That was very nice, but it doesn't answer my questions, now does it?"

"No, but you taste good." His dad looked at him when he cleared his throat. "I'm sorry. But yes, the little dragon touched you. It was to help you heal from what they did to you. You were set on dying, and they knew, even before me, what you were to me and mine. I told you, I'm getting straight now, but it's taking me a few minutes."

Emerald pulled Chase up from the couch. They were leaving the room when he heard Brandy giggle. It was nice, he supposed, but also a little strange. His dad had a mate. Not just any mate either, but a slightly human almost vampire one. This was going to be fun, Chase thought. A stepmom that was decades and decades younger than he was.

~~~

Emerald sat at the table at the warehouse that Jewel owned. This was the fourth day in a row that she'd been there, and she didn't think things were going any better today than they had when she had worked there. The building was coming along, yes. And they were sending out product now, but the employees were no less afraid of the owners than they had been before. It was hurting all of them not to be trusted.

Translating what was being said in three different languages was also taking its toll on her. Not only were they of different nationalities, but also different dialects. Emerald had finally had enough. Standing up on the table, she looked over the group of people there and pressed magic around them.

"Can you all understand me?" Every one of them nodded, and she looked at Jewel. "I should have done this from the start. Okay, go ahead and tell them again what is going to happen with this place. And please, for the love of dragons, don't mention that you will need to get them green cards again."

Jewel nodded at her as she stood up on the table beside her. Even as the questions came to her, Emerald knew that things were going to go much better, and a good deal faster. They could all understand each other, and nothing was lost in the translation.

The plant was doing very well. Not only were they hiring a great many people that otherwise wouldn't be able to work because of different reasons, Jewel had made it easier on the elderly that only wanted to work a day or two a week. And some of her employees had babysitting issues that Jewel made sure were worked around as well.

Jewel had even made it easier for some of the people to get their education. It was just high school level, but it was more of a chance than most of the people had had before. Hot meals were provided, as well as minor medical care if someone was sick or needed stitches, even if it hadn't been a work-related injury. That was where Emerald was headed now, to the infirmary, not to the offices, where she knew that Kristie would normally be. The woman was going to need bubble wrap if this kept up. She'd been taken to see the doctor just half an hour ago.

"Hello, Kristie, how's it going?" Kristie was becoming a big part of this place, and Emerald was glad for it. She was nice, and she had a positive attitude that made her smile. "I thought you were going to set up your office today. I know that you had help."

"Yes, well, I banged my ankle on the chair, and this guy said that I have to have it looked at." She said ouch when he touched his fingers to the bump. "Jamie is going to have a fit. I promised him that I'd be careful, and now look. I have a bruise that he is going to notice for sure."

Emerald touched her fingers to the wound and helped her stand up. She needed her for a few moments, and having her going for x-rays wasn't going to help her. Kristie asked her what she'd done.

"I healed it. I can do small things like that, fix wounds that might require stitches or such. I needed you now, not in a few

119

hours. I have noticed that humans can take a very long time in a place that is supposed to help you heal." Kristie laughed, and Emerald felt her own smile tug at her lips. "You are very nice. I do hope people figure that out about you quickly."

"It might take them a little bit, but they get around to it. What did you need? I'm assuming that since you healed me and brought me here to my offices, that you need something legal done?" Emerald sat down and nodded. "Please tell me that it's not going to be something like you need a contract taken out on someone. Or that you want to sue a drug manufacturing company because they made you hear things."

"You're getting that here?" Kristie nodded, and laughed when she did. "No. I have some funds that I'd like for you to add Chase to. Much of it is just investments. I also have a few homes that I rent out when someone wants a vacation."

"Really? I guess if you're around for a long time, you can get deals on stuff like ocean front property. Jamie and I want to do that sometime. Invest like that. Right now...well, never mind. I can do that for you. Just let me know the names of the investments and the properties, and I can get right on that." Emerald started to ask her what she had started to say, but Kristie continued before she could. "I have to take the board here, which I'm to do soon. After that, I can get a start on everything you need. But until then, all I'll need to do is file the paperwork and you'll be set. I have things here for you to sign as well. Chase has done the same thing for you."

Emerald knew that he'd done that. He'd told her today that she needed to go by and sign some forms. She also knew his net worth, as he did hers. Emerald had been around longer, and her savings were a good deal more, but it mattered little to either of them, so long as they had enough money to use to help people. Like, she was beginning to think, the person in front of her.

How much are we paying Kristie to work for us? Chase said that he didn't know, that Grayson had set it up. *I'm thinking that whatever it is, we need to seriously look into giving them more. I don't think they're struggling, not really, but they have a baby coming soon, and until the pay kicks in for Jamie, I think they might be a little tight. Especially if she has to take time off. I bet she doesn't realize that we're paying her full pay while she's off, either. We are, aren't we?*

I'll ask him. I do know that the house that they're living in is a rental. I don't know what the rent is, but now that you mention it, there should be no cost to that either. We own the house and the things in it. She asked him where their things were. *They didn't have anything much. His parents collected rent from them. The furnishings that were in the house, I heard, belonged to them as well. I got the feeling from the moving company that they stood over them when they were there, making sure that they only packed what belonged to them. And get this, I don't think they're very happy about the baby either.*

Fuckers. It was a word that she'd heard used over and over by Ryan, Chase's brother when he was talking about something or someone. She thought in this instance, it worked well. *They need something of their own. And they need to be able to use any of our homes abroad when they want. I mean, none of your family has to do that. I don't know what they might even have, but between the two of us, we can let them tour the world and never have to pay out for a place to stay.*

All right. I like that idea. And to get them to go, which I'm thinking might be harder than you'd believe, we'll say that they have to check out the properties so that we can have a good eye on them. That way, it'll seem less like they're sponging off us, and they will think it's a working vacation. She told him he was brilliant. *Yes, well, you bring that out in me. Also, we have to go before the vampire board and tell them why we killed six of the new vamps. They know*

121

why, but they need to make this formal. Jason is in charge of this realm, but he can't be a part of this, being my brother and all.

All right, I can do that. I know most of them anyway. She had helped form the board, as a matter of fact. *I have to finish up here, and then I have one more stop to make. It's about Bates. He's in the hospital, and I need to make it clear to him, somehow, that I'm not going to tolerate him trying to capture me. He might live longer if he backs off.*

Do you think that'll work? She told him it was worth a try. *Yes, well, so long as you don't expect too much from it. He seems like a man that is set on doing things his way.*

After getting the things done she needed with Kristie, she set Soto to stay with her today. She didn't want her to over extend herself, and Emerald had a feeling that she would, simply because she liked what she was doing. Soto said he'd take good care of her.

On her way to the hospital, she heard from Grayson. He said that he'd not thought of how things were so tight without the extra income of Jamie, and would double her pay. Also, he said the family was going to help them get a house and furnishings. All in all, she hoped that the rest of her day was just as good. But she knew, somehow, that it wouldn't be.

Chapter 10

Harold thought about looking around the big emergency room. He'd been in here before. He'd been handcuffed like some kind of criminal, and had let them know how unfair it was. But this time, with his head pounding like someone was taking a rock to it, he didn't. Not that he didn't have a great deal to complain about, but his head aching kept him from being too loud about it.

When his nose itched, he pulled his hand up and scratched it. He was just putting his hand back on the bed when he realized that he wasn't cuffed. Moving his other hand, just enough to test the waters, so to speak, he was happy to find out he was free. But that still left his feet, so he gingerly moved them and found they too were free of shackles.

"Mr. Bates, I'm going to stitch up your head now." He didn't so much as nod at her. He knew that he was safe from her seeing his face; the large blue paper-like thing over him prevented that. "I guess he's still out. Did you want me to wait or just go ahead and fix this?"

"Do it. I don't have time to wait on his ass all day. Stitch his wound up, and then I'll take him back to his cell.

Hopefully he'll remain out and I can have some peace and quiet for a change." The woman laughed, and he knew that it was the officer that had given him such a hard time when he was incarcerated. "I have never known a man that was so set in the late forties before. He has the mentality of a man twice his age when it comes to women in the workplace."

It was on the tip of his tongue to tell her that his way was the way it should have been, but kept it to himself. If he was going to be able to get out of here soon, he'd have to keep his opinions to himself. There was work afoot, and he needed to not be in here to get it done.

He didn't feel the pain in his head after the initial pin prick. Harold figured that they'd not numb his head, just to be mean to him. But after she was done, which seemed to him took entirely too long, he heard the two of them leave the room.

It was imperative that he get out of here now. He knew that he'd not get another chance, not with the way things were going for him of late. Just as he pulled the paper off his face, he knew that it was time to move. He was alone in the cubical, and the door was standing wide open.

Standing proved to be a bit more difficult than he had thought it should have been. But once he was steady enough to get going, he grabbed his shoes from under the bed and made his way out of the curtained off area toward the door.

They were busy, thankfully. And he wasn't stopped once on his way to freedom. However, almost as soon as he was near enough to see outside, two officers came in with a man between them. He was screaming bloody murder and telling them they had the wrong guy when Harold moved back, just leaned against the wall like he belonged there.

As soon as they were gone, he went out into the cold. It was both refreshing and painful. Slipping on his shoes, he realized that he didn't have a coat, and shivered a couple of times as he made his way to the hotel. He figured that he had just about enough time to get there and out before anyone in this town noticed that he was gone. They were stupid enough to leave him alone and uncuffed, after all. So in his mind, they were getting what they deserved.

It took him far longer than he thought it should to find the hotel he'd been staying in. But as soon as he saw it, he knew that he wasn't going to get his things. The place was surrounded by cops, and they were walking around like they were set to stay. As one more pulled up in front of the place, he saw an opportunity that he just could not let go. Reaching into the car, he not only was rewarded with a coat, but also a handgun.

"If these idiots worked for me, then I'd have all their asses on the line. Or fired." He pulled the coat up over his jacket and was disturbed by the slight smell. The person who had worn this item must have one of those wives that liked to spread their perfume all over themselves, then hug their husbands as they went out the door. "I have to smell like a whore all day now."

Harold moved between the buildings to watch what they were doing, and wasn't surprised to see them talking it up and acting like there was nothing amiss. He was a wanted man, he was sure, yet none of them seemed to be in the least bit of a hurry to bring him in. Then he saw her.

She was sitting on one of the cars, her coat discarded at some point, yet she looked to be as warm as toast sitting there. It was then that he realized she was looking right at him, as if she knew he was lurking about. Instead of coming after him, as he thought she might, or even warning the others he was there, she saluted him. Like he was getting away, simply because she was allowing it.

Harold watched her as she sat there, wondering what anyone would do if he were to aim his gun at her and fire. But when he felt a pain in his head, he paused in lifting it up. There was a fear that was there now, and he knew that she'd been responsible for planting it there. Harold wasn't sure how she'd done it, but he was positive that it had been her.

You have balls, I'll give you that. What other person do you know that would return to the scene of the crime like you have? He looked around for the person who spoke to him and wondered where they were. *It's me, Bates. Emma Green, I think you might know me by. You've fucked up badly, so you know. However did you get away with this shit when you were working for the Bureau?*

"How are you doing this?" She laughed then, a hardy laugh that made his skin crawl and his balls tighten to his body. "How are you speaking to me from over there? Is this some sort of trick? Do you have a speaker here?"

I'm magical. And if you don't want to have your ass hauled back to jail right now, I would suggest that you speak to me as I am you. Just think of what you want to say. That'll work. He didn't want to try that. That would mean that she had some sort of power over him. And Harold didn't want anyone, especially a woman, having anything over him.

I don't believe you. Yet when he spoke to her, he knew that she could understand and hear him while the others did not. *You have had them plant something in my head when they stitched me up. That's it, isn't it? Who told you how to do this? Your boss? The one that made you like you are? Who is he?*

No, I didn't. If I would have wanted them to plant something in your head, it might have been a brain. I think yours is somewhere in the vicinity of your ass. And no one taught this to me. I was created this way. As a dragon warrior. He started to lift the gun, thinking to end her life now. *You try that, Bates, and you'll never pull the trigger.*

126

He put the gun in his pocket. It was much too tempting to use it on her. Having it put away like it was, he thought he could try and have a conversation with her that didn't end in her death. He needed the man who had done this to her.

I have come all this way to talk to you. I have an idea that you're given some sort of medicine or herb that makes you appear young. Is that it, there is a drug you take? She told him no. *Then how is it possible that you can be the same woman you have been throughout the decades? I have aged, why haven't you?*

Because, as I said, I'm magical. What I don't understand is how you can believe that I can be immortal, yet not that I could be talking to you in your head. By the way, do you know that most of the people who work with you aren't human either? He told her that wasn't possible. He'd had all his men screened. *Being a paranormal won't show up on a screening, you moron. They have to have someone sniff them out, or better yet, tell you that they're not human. Or a vampire. That's what my mate is. A vampire. The entire Crosby family is.*

You lie. She shrugged, and he wanted to kill her right then and there. *Come back with me. Tell me how you have been able to be ageless, and who the person is that did this for you. And I don't for a moment believe that you're immortal. You can be killed like anyone else can.*

Nope. I have been around for centuries. Fought in wars that you would have read about, some you might never know. I have used more magic than most people are aware of, and I command dragons to do as I wish. He told her there was no such thing as dragons. *Again, you have a strange and screwed up way of thinking. Yes, there are dragons. And vampires, as well as faeries and brownies. There is even a pack of unicorns on the queen of faeries land that are so beautiful that they hurt your heart when you see them.*

Why must you say things like that? Are you trying your best to piss me off? Everyone knows that there are no such things as faeries.

127

Nor are there things like wolves that can change into men. And I cannot believe that you would even think I'd believe that there are things such as dragons. She told him to look to his left. *Why, are there things that go bump in the night?*

Laughing at his own joke, he turned to his left. A man stood there, one that he'd not seen before, and when he tipped his hat to him, he changed. The big wolf standing in his place made Harold think of all the horror movies he'd ever seen. Then in the blink of an eye, he was a man again.

Shaking, he knew that she was saying his name. But at least for the moment, he could do nothing more than just make himself breathe in and out. When he turned to look at her again, he felt destroyed. His entire thought process was gone, because all his thoughts and beliefs had gone straight out the window.

Now, I want you to look at the building just a little to the right of the man. Once you do, then I want you to tell me again how there are no such things as dragons. He looked, his mind already ready for the lie—hoping for it actually—to be made when there sat a large silver dragon. When he spread his wings, knocking against the building to his right, Harold backed up, sure he was going to be fried with his hot breath. *He's not a fire breathing dragon, but an ice one. Mine, as a matter of fact. And being mine, I can have him breathe his ice over you and you'd be dead even before he disappeared again. You're very lucky that you've caught me on a good day. But that, Mr. Bates, is the very thing that you don't believe in. A dragon as big as…well, bigger than life.*

A good day? He was still staring at the dragon; there had to be some sort of trickery going on. He wasn't sure what it might be, but there wasn't anything like dragons on this earth. *What is that supposed to mean?*

When he turned back to her, she was standing inches

from him. Backing up quickly, his feet tangled up and he fell on his ass, but instead of taking the hand that she offered him, he stared up at her. The pictures that he had hadn't done her justice at all.

The woman was beyond beautiful. Her skin was as smooth looking as a porcelain vase. Her eyes, the color of green, were so vivid, so intense, that he had to blink several times to bring them in focus. But it was the suit of armor that she wore that terrified him. So much so that he crab-walked back from her.

"You should come with me." She asked him why she'd do that. "I need to get my job back and take care that people aren't murdered in their sleep by something like you. I don't know what you are, but you're a danger to John Q. Public, and we both know that."

"You really need to work on your bedside manner. And no, I'm not going anywhere with you. I have some rules for you that I know for a fact that you're not going to follow. But I did promise my husband that I'd give them to you anyway. I want you to stay away from Jamie and his wife." He asked who that was. "Nash. Stay away from them. Also, stop this foolishness of trying to take me in. It's not going to happen. I'm smarter than you. And I have a great deal of magic on my side, not to mention the dragons. Go retire or whatever it is you need to do, but stay out of my life and those of my family."

"If, as you say, these things are real, I believe that I need to have my job back so that I can capture them and put them in a lab." She knelt to his level and he could see the anger in her eyes. Harold could almost taste it, it was that obvious to him. "You're not going to be able to kill me, my dear. Women of your ilk, they don't kill men as often as you'd think."

She touched her fingers to his head. The pain was incredible. Screaming out with it, he saw the blade being drawn, the way it ran through him. Then he was lifted up, his body slicing along his torso like warm butter. When he was stuck to the building behind him, he knew as surely as he was hanging there that he was dead. Coughing before he could speak, he felt the spittle of blood run down his chin. Then... then nothing.

Harold rubbed his chest where the blade had been... it had been so real that he was sure that he had been cut. Wiping at his mouth, there wasn't any blood there, not even a small drop. And the woman was gone. Not even the police were around the hotel now. The dragon and the wolf had also disappeared, and he was alone again. Standing, he thought of how ridiculous it had been for him to have believed her when he turned to go to the hotel again.

"Boo." She was suddenly there, her face masked in the armor that she had on.

Screaming as he fell back, Harold reached for her and felt his hands grow cold from touching her. She had tricked him. He wasn't sure how, but she had done this to him, and he was going to make her pay.

As his head was hitting the wall behind him, pain rattled through his entire body. And just before he fainted, the pain was that harsh, he heard her laughter, and knew that it had all been real, and he was only seeing a glimpse of what she was going to do to him.

~~~

Brandy wasn't sure what she was supposed to do. First of all, they were really friendly, but she just didn't feel like she fit in with them. While they were loud and boisterous, she was quiet and reserved. When Franklin sat beside her, she took his offered hand like a lifeline. He kissed the back of it and asked her if she was all right.

"I don't know. Should I be?" He laughed, and she felt it

all over her body like a warmed blanket. "I don't know them. And if one more of your sons calls me mom, I'm going to murder him in his sleep. What are they, a couple of hundred years older than me?"

"More than that, I'm afraid." She asked him how old he was. "Let me think on that for a moment. I haven't thought of my age in more years than I think you've been around."

"You're not funny." He laughed. "But really, aren't they very old? I mean, to be having a mother figure in their lives?"

"Jason is my oldest. He was born right after his mother and I came together. He was born in the year twelve hundred or so. The rest of them, they came along about a hundred years or less after him." She looked at Jason, who was holding his wife like she was a piece of glass that he treasured more than he did himself. "When their mother was killed, it was all I could do not to join her. But the boys, men by then, I guess, needed me. So I hung around. Then when Kilian gave us this special gift, I wasn't able to join her, so I was upset about that for a very long time. Until one of them pointed it out to me recently. Since then, especially since you've joined me, I've been thinking about life a lot differently. Happier, I guess you could say."

"How long has your wife been gone?" He told her what her name had been. "Rena. That's lovely. When did she pass away?"

"Just about the time that our youngest had come into his own. As a full-blooded vampire, he was about twenty-five or so. Not very old by comparison. He more than likely doesn't even remember her. I know that I have a hard time with it at times." Brandy told him she was sorry. "No need for it. But she didn't pass away, like you think. Some humans, they tied her to the ground and let the sun take her. I had to stand by and watch her, knowing that if I were to try and save her,

I'd be just as dead. But, like I said, my sons needed me, so I didn't. Plus, they held me back. It was a horrific death for anyone, but to watch her, it tore me up for a long time."

"But that won't hurt you now? The sun I mean?" He said that it wouldn't, then told her about how they'd stayed in the sun an entire day when they'd first been given this gift and had gotten sunburned. How they had eaten real food too, and had been sickened by it since they'd never had it before. "I bet that was a wonderful feeling for you all. To have the sun on your faces."

"It was. It surely was." He looked around the room as he continued. "I've been a very lucky man in my life. Good boys to care for me when I need it. A home and enough to eat. We've not had a great deal of use for money, not before nor much afterwards, but it's been handy. And we do what we can with what we have to make things comfortable for us and the good people in the town. We've all been very lucky."

"Says a man who has it all." She tried to laugh with him, but she didn't have two nickels to rub together. "I don't know what to do, Franklin. I like you a great deal and I feel safe with you, but I haven't any idea what to do about being with a vampire, much less a family of them."

"What would you be doing right now if you didn't have a care in the world?" She asked him if he meant money. "That too. I mean, if you could do something, something just for yourself, what would you be doing?"

"When I was ten, I wanted my passport so badly that I saved all my baby-sitting money for an entire year. I didn't have the money to go anywhere, but my plans had been to run away and see the world." She laughed. "I had no idea that having my passport would require so much from my parents. They told me that I wasn't going to be able to go anywhere, so I might as well just forget it. They wouldn't even help me out with a dream. I think that is why this trip I was on meant so much to me. No passport, of course, but traveling around was fun. And educational too."

"You want to travel? I haven't been anywhere in a long time, but I'd like to do that as well. See the world for the first time in your eyes." She stared at him, sure he was kidding. "We can leave whenever you want. Today should you want. I know a few people, and we can get you a passport today if you decide where we'll go first."

"I don't.... Are you serious? Just up and go?" He nodded at her, and she thought of all the things she didn't have that would be required of one traveling. "I don't know, Franklin. What about the house we're supposed to look at tomorrow? And I've yet to get my things from my apartment sorted out."

"We'll buy what we need when we need it. Take only what we can carry and a credit card. Which reminds me. I had this fixed for you today." Franklin handed her a fistful of credit cards, all of them with her name on them. Brandy Crosby. "I know that I've not asked you yet to marry me...I meant too, but you're just so damned beautiful that I forget myself. Will you be my wife, Brandy? Make me happy and travel the world with me?"

"Yes. Yes, I will." Giggling, something that she'd never done before now, she kissed Franklin when he kissed her. She loved him. Right then, it occurred to her that she loved him. "I love you, Franklin."

"Hot damn." She was embarrassed when he shouted to the room. The people all quieted down, and Franklin went down on one knee in front of her. "Brandy, will you please say it again and then tell me yes, you'll marry me?"

"I love you, Franklin Crosby, and yes, I'll marry you." Everyone cheered then. It was the first time that she really enjoyed all the noise. And there was a great deal of it too.

By the time they were entering the big dining room, Brandy was giddy with happiness. Franklin told them that they were going to honeymoon by seeing the world, and that they'd be back when they ran out of places to see. Calls were made, and the family plane was put on hold for them to use for the next few days. After that, they'd be traveling first class.

"You're happy?" She nodded at Jewel, and felt like she'd gained a good friend in her. "I'm so glad. Franklin has been so lonely lately, I think. And Jason said he's ever seen him so happy before."

"I am as well. I have been alone most of my life, even when I was living with my parents." Jewel told her she was sorry. "Don't be. Had they been nicer, I might not have gotten out on my own and.... Well, meeting up with the other vampires was terribly scary, but I got to meet all of you as well, and I think I'm going to see this as a win."

"Good for you."

As they passed around food, Chase and Emerald had their cook, Dustin, tell them about himself. He was a good man, Emerald had told them, and they welcomed him into their family just as they had her. This was, she thought, the strangest and the most romantic dinner she'd ever eaten. And she was happy too. Something that she never in her life thought she'd be.

Chapter 11

"I'm sorry sir, but I cannot allow you to stay here without a credit card and identification card. That is company policy." Harold had decided that he'd get further along if he didn't mention that he was an agent anymore. Plus, he had to stop using his cards and his driver's license for things, like checking into a hotel. "I understand that you do have cash to pay for things, but we need a credit card number on file in the event that something happens, and we need to reimburse you for it."

"Reimburse me for what? I only want to stay a couple of nights, then move on. I want a shower and food." The man shook his head. "I'm getting mightily tired of being treated this way."

"Sir, lower your voice or I'll call in security." He growled low, but the man must have had his hearing aids turned up all the way, because he told him there would be none of that either. "You cannot stay here without proper identification. If there is nothing else, then I have other clients to care for."

He stood there for as long as he could, but there wasn't any budging some people. Harold could stay in the little

135

dive down the road for as long as he wanted and for nearly a third of the price. But he wanted clean sheets against his skin. Towels that were soft as could be obtained, and more than that, he wanted a breakfast that was wonderfully prepared and not out of a box or bag.

But it wasn't to be. He was a wanted man. A man on the run. While it did have a strange sound to it, him being an agent and all, he wasn't happy with the way things were going for him, nor happy at all with anyone.

As he made his way to the cheaper and probably much dirtier hotel, the woman spoke to him again. She'd been doing that all damned day, and he was getting sick of it. Telling her to stop had no effect on her either. Even threatening her, zip. Harold was sure she was going to have him up all night too.

There is a faerie following you. She said to tell you that if you want clean sheets, for you to go home. He didn't answer her this time. Engaging with her only made her talk more. *And, so you know, don't judge a book by its cover. It's rude, and usually you're wrong.*

How the hell would you know? Damn it, he thought, he had opened a can of words again with her. *Leave me alone. I have better things to do than to be talking to you all the time.*

Do you? I think not. So far, you've turned your nose up at the newspaper that was lying on the counter for anyone to read because you'd not read it first. Complained about the coffee that you were served, saying that it was too weak. You didn't leave a tip, not one cent to the waitress you made cry. It wasn't her fault that you ordered an over easy egg and the yolk wasn't up to your standards. Runny is runny if you ask me. If those are productive to you, then it's no wonder that you're on the lam. He had made the little girl cry, and he'd enjoyed it too. *You're not a nice person. I'm positive that people have told you that before, but it bore pointing out again.*

I'm not a bad person, but one that enjoys rules and having things done the right way. No one takes as much pride in what they do as I do. The world is in ruination if you ask me because of this way of thinking. She asked him if evading the police was one of his rules. *I did nothing wrong, so I don't feel that I was properly arrested.*

Properly? I don't know what you mean by that, but there was just cause in arresting you. You insulted that doctor. You hurt those –

We are not going to go into this again, are we? I swear, you're like a never-ending record. Just going on and on all the time. I didn't hurt anyone. I also didn't insult that woman. She is a female, and there is no position that a woman can hold that she'd be any good at, unless it's running a household. Emma, or whatever her name was, asked him if that included children. *You mean raising them? Of course. That's what they were put on this earth for.*

You're such a dick head. He said nothing. *You do know that a woman raised you to be.... Wait, that's not a good reference. Your mother should be shot for raising you like you are. You're a bastard and a chauvinistic prick. Why on earth don't you read a newspaper or even watch a movie that has color in it? You'd see that you're so far behind in the times that you might have to have a backhoe to dig you out to this century.*

Harold asked for a room that was clean, and the man behind the counter only stared at him. After telling him that he wanted a room that had a large shower and thick towels, he was asked if he wanted his breakfast served to him in bed too. Harold asked him if he was serious, excited to have something done for him in a proper way.

"No, I'm not serious. What would make you think I'd bring you breakfast in bed? Christ love a duck, I don't even feed my wife in bed, even if she don't feel well." He corrected his wording of the sentence. "Are you a teacher or something? If not, then shut the fuck up and go to your room."

"No, as a matter of fact, I'm an FBI agent here on a job." The man just snorted at him and handed him the key. "Aren't you the least bit impressed that you have an agent staying in your hotel?"

"Nope. So long as the money is good, you can call yourself J. Edgar Hoover for all I care. Room three." He took the key and thought about telling the man that J. Edgar Hoover had been an agent too, but decided that he'd not care. Or he more than likely thought that the man had invented the vacuum or some such thing.

As he made his way to the room, he looked around. There was a large ice machine under an awning. Several of the rooms had chairs out front of them, like they had nothing better to do with their time than to watch cars pull in and out of the lot. Opening the door, he nearly backed out when he turned on the light.

The carpet was purple. Not just like a light color that you might mistake for purple, but gleaming bright purple, with specs of glitter, it looked like, in it. He was almost afraid of what the rest of the room looked like when he stepped inside and looked around.

"Holy mother of God." The spread on the bed was equally purple. No glitter this time, but the design on it, paisley he thought, was nauseating. As the black lines seemed to move over it, he sat down on the room's chair.

The dresser was painted the same color, with small pebbles of glass on the top that were both black and the purple color. The walls were striped too, the alternating colors so close together that he thought for sure that a blind person would had to have hung the wallpaper. It would have been too much to see this stuff moving while carrying it to the wall.

The bathroom, or what he could see of it, had the same shower curtain pattern as the spread. The towels were folded up and laying on an equally adorned rack that sparkled when he moved his head a certain way. The floor, thankfully only white, along with the commode, was stark against the rest of the things in the room. Harold wondered if he should ask for another room, but decided that he might end up in something putrid colored, or maybe even all the colors in the rainbow. He turned off the light, hoping that it would be easier on the eyes. It wasn't. Some of the things glowed.

The pebbles glowed to the point where he had to cover his eyes when he moved by it. The spread, too, had some sort of light in it that made the paisley look like it was moving. There were stickers on the ceiling too. He had no idea what the intended design should have been, but he had to turn the lights back on or be deathly ill from it. Harold knew that the woman was responsible for this mess, and he made a mental note not to mention it to her. So she'd think it hadn't phased him at all.

Putting away his few things, he didn't look around anymore. It was dizzying to do that and try to stand upright. The room was making him ill, and he wasn't up to having to try and figure out if he could throw up in the toilet without seeing purple sparkles coming out of him.

Putting on his only other clean shirt, he decided to try the little dive across the street from the hotel. There were a lot of cars in the lot...a few semis as well. And since he'd had to skip breakfast and lunch, he was starving enough to sit in one of the nasty booths. As soon as he entered, he could smell the food.

"Howdy. You all by yourself tonight?" Telling the waitress that he was alone, he followed as she took him to a table. There were a lot of people enjoying their meals, and he felt his belly growl at the sights and smells that were coming his way. As soon as he was seated, she brought him a cup of coffee.

The menu was a sheet of laminated paper that had tonight's, Saturday's, meals on it. It wasn't sticky, like he thought it would be, nor was there anything much on the thing that he'd want to eat. Settling for an open-faced turkey sandwich, whatever that was, he sipped his coffee and was surprised at how delicious it was.

In less than five minutes he had not only rolls with warmed butter, but cream in a pitcher, as well as honey should he want it. Harold didn't care all that much for breads, but once he saw the steam billowing from the basket, he tried one so he could complain about how dry it was. Or find out that they'd microwaved it to make it hot and it was now hard and tasteless. He could not have been more wrong. It was like eating wonderfully warm slices of heaven. Bread, in all his life, had never tasted nearly this good before.

Harold nearly fell out of his chair when he was served his dinner. There was thick slabs of bread with turkey all over it. He found that there was stuffing too, between the bread sandwich, as well as the creamiest mashed potatoes he'd ever eaten. The gravy, as far as he was concerned, was a national treasure. He was in heaven. Until someone sat down with him. Three people, as it turned out.

"Mr. Bates." The first man took his plate and asked for a clean fork, while the second man asked for some pie. They argued over what kind, and simply had the waitress bring them a slice of all of them. When she was gone again the man eating his dinner asked if one of the other two wanted a bite.

"That is my dinner you're eating." He said nothing to him, but did lay a gun on the table. Just put it there like that would settle any arguments from him. "What do you want? Besides my dinner."

"We were sent here by Grayson. And Elliot, but Grayson

contacted us first. Have you met them? The Crosby men? They're a good bunch, but not very friendly when it comes to people like you." Harold asked him what that was supposed to mean. "The kind that gets themselves killed and no one finds the body kind of person."

~~~

Emerald had never thought of how nice and wonderfully relaxing a hot tub could be. Her muscles felt like they were gooey, and her feet had long since decided that she was never leaving this space.

"I would have thought, you having the need to heal in a freezer, the hot tub would be a no-no for you." Chase joined her in the tub and sighed heavily. "This is very nice. I've had it for some time, just never got around to using it. How do you like it?"

"I'm not leaving." He laughed. "Seriously, my muscles have gone on strike. I can't even lift my head up."

He slid closer to her and lifted her up so that she was on his lap, their legs tangled together. She was naked, as was he, and she loved that he didn't immediately try and make love to her, but did touch her. It was comforting as well as sexy.

"I've been thinking about a couple of different things. One was the way you're trying to make Bates insane. I love that. He can tell the truth, yet not be believed by anyone that he speaks to." She told him that she'd used it once before, this plan of hers, and it had worked out well. "I like that he won't have to be injured unless he continues to fuck up."

"Yes. He's not really evil, just stupid. And stubborn." Chase agreed with her on that assessment as well. "And the second thing you've been thinking about?"

"Children. And before you say yes or no, I want to tell you a few things. I don't know how to tell if you're in heat. Or even if you do go into heat. For all I know, you could be

141

carrying my child right now." She told him she wasn't, and saw the flash of sadness as he continued. "We've never talked about them. Having them or not. But I'd like to have a child with you. Whenever you're ready."

"You won't have any say in when I'm ready?" He explained to her what he'd meant. "So you're saying that even though you'd love to have me fat with your child, you won't tell me when because it's my body."

"Yes. I mean, it is yours, and even though I'd have a blast creating a child with you, I'm not the one that would be going through the most difficult thing in my life like you would be." She nodded, understanding what he meant. "Also, I'm pretty sure that I won't ever want to tell you that you should do anything you don't want to. You have dragons to call upon."

Turning, Emerald sat on his lap and felt his cock stretch and thicken between them. Kissing him, making him as much aware of her as she was him, she lifted her head just enough that she could look him in his eyes and kiss him again if she wanted.

"I want children with you. But, before you say yes or no, you must realize that I'm a far superior being than you are, and the likelihood of any of our kids being only a vampire is pretty slim." He smiled at her. "They might not even be a vampire at all, but just an ice warrior."

"I can live with that, so long as the little girls are as beautiful as you, and the little boys are as kick ass as their mother." She loved him for that. "However, I'd very much like to, if you don't mind, name a daughter for my mom."

"Rena." Chase nodded. "Yes, I would love that. It's a very pretty name. It means Peaceful. Which, knowing the two of us and the rest of this family, it's doubtful that she would be."

"I hope not. I want her or any of them to be just as brave and as happy as we are. You are happy, aren't you, Emerald?"

She nodded, overwhelmed with emotion just then. "I love you, so very much."

"And I you." She lifted herself up with his help and slid down over his cock. He filled her, in ways that didn't just mean her body, but her heart and soul as well. "We can have a child, now if you'd like."

Chase rolling his hips made her moan. And when he suckled at her breast, she held him to her as she took her own pleasure. He let her, too, riding him in long and quick strokes until she was so close that she could almost touch it. And when he bit down on her nipple and suckled hard, she knew a kind of pleasure that made her cry out that she was coming and released hard.

"Again, love. Come on me again while I feed from you." Emerald couldn't have stopped herself from coming had she a blade at her throat. It felt wonderfully fulfilling to have a man feed from her as he gave her the most incredible pleasure.

When he lifted her out of the hot water, he never stopped giving her as much as she wanted. Even though her body was chilled, he warmed it up right away with his mouth and touch. As he sat her on the side of the tub, she wrapped her legs around him, renewed now with a need to have him fill her.

"Give me your child." He nodded, kissing her mouth almost savagely. "Please, Chase. I need it, I need you."

He exploded inside of her. Not just filling her womb with his babe, but her body too. All of her seemed to have received some part of him, whether it was just his love or something more, something magical. And when he bit deeply into her throat, she cried out again, holding him to her until she was able to fill him as well.

He took her up to their room after that. She could have walked, she supposed, but having him carry her, his cock still deep within her, she loved being with him. As he laid her on the bed, his mouth doing incredible things to her own, Emerald rose and fell with each of his strokes, and fell more deeply in love with Chase than she ever thought possible.

When she came this time, it was gentle, like he was spreading her with his love rather than just making love to her, and the ease to fall asleep took her under. When she closed her eyes, Emerald knew that when she woke, if she needed him, Chase would forever be there.

"I love you, Emerald." Nodding, she was unable to speak she was so relaxed. His soft laughter made her smile. "Had I known I could render you speechless by putting you in the hot tub, I might have used it long ago."

She didn't care that he teased her. Emerald couldn't care less if he were to roll her to her back and leave her nakedly exposed to the world. She was in love, and loved in return. There wasn't anything in this world that could make her feel any better than that.

When the noises in the room woke her, she looked up to see that Soto was there, speaking to Chase. Asking what was going on, they both assured her that it was all right, and she closed her eyes again. Sleep took her under once again. Emerald was sure that whatever was going on, the two of them could handle it better than she could right now.

Chapter 12

Chase wasn't really positive if he could do this, much less if he should. He knew that he'd been told that he was the king of the dragons, but even with that knowledge, he wasn't sure. Not to mention the knowledge that had come with the crown when he'd had it placed on his head had been running in circles for days now, but bringing a dragon to justice was harder than he thought it would be.

"Your lordship, I didn't mean to cause any trouble." For some reason, he had an idea that the dragon was lying. Not only that, but he was hiding more than just this trouble from him. "I will be better in the future, you can count on me."

He has lied to you twice now, my lord. Soto was sitting on his shoulder, holding onto his ear lobe like he'd seen him do with Emerald. *He has walked this path before, on numerous occasions, while there was no one to hold him accountable.*

Chase asked why he hadn't been, and was told that without anyone in charge, it had been hard. So now, Chase would bet, since there was someone to hold the dragons to the rules, they'd see this a great deal more.

"You have not only shown yourself to the human world,

145

but you have also destroyed a big part of their livelihood." Chase knew that he'd help the couple who had lost their business because of this dragon's actions, but these people had seen him do it. "You have endangered not only all dragons, but me and my family as well. I don't think that you telling me that you'll be good from now on will suffice."

"No, you see, that's okay. I said I'd not do it again, and that's the end of it. You'll see. I'll be a model dragon from now on." Soto snorted. "You be quiet. No one asked you. But I'll just go back to my cave and think about what I've done. I'll be good. You'll see."

"No, this isn't the end of it. From what I'm to understand, you've done and said this before. That you'd not do it again, and here we are, visiting the same behavior as before." He nodded, and Chase had a feeling that it had worked for him in the past, agreeing and just going about his business as usual. "You are to work on the building that you destroyed. Human money, all that they lose during the reconstruction, will be repaid to them from you. As well as—"

"No, I don't think you're understanding how sorry I am. Plus, I told you that I'd think on what I'd done. It won't happen again. No, you can bet on that." Chase told him to do as he'd said and tried to finish the dragon's punishment. "If I have to pay them out of my wages, which I don't have any, then how will I live? I mean, you're talking a great deal of human money."

"So I am, and perhaps the next time you do something this stupid, you'll think on that. In addition to the wages and helping them rebuild, if you are caught again doing such a thing, especially being seen by the human fold, then you will leave me no choice but to sentence you to death." The dragon just stared at him for a full minute before he laughed. Loudly. "You think my punishment is funny? That my words have so little meaning to you that you'd scoff at them?"

"You can't kill me. I know that you're the king and all, but we all know that you, as a non-warrior, don't have it within you to kill a creature such as I. And there are so very few of us left. Killing me would be a bad thing to do." Chase asked him how he'd come to that conclusion. "You aren't the type of man to do that. Not to mention, you cannot kill something as rare as myself. I'm a dragon. That alone should be enough to keep you from destroying me. It's the way things have always been done."

By now they'd gathered a group of the others. No one seemed to be disagreeing with the dragon, but they didn't seem to be agreeing with him either. Several of them, Soto told him, had had this particular dragon harm some of their own things as well.

"Well, think of this as being under new management. I'm telling you what you're to do, and if you don't do it, I won't have any other choice but to destroy you. I won't want to, but you'll leave me no choice in the matter." The dragon was nodding again, thinking that he was off the hook, no doubt. "Now, as for the monies that this family is going to need."

"You aren't going to get any of my things for them. I have been around a very long time, even before you. I won't give up my things just because I've had me some fun." He looked around at the rest of the group of dragons. There were faeries and brownies as well, but they all just stood there. "Ask them. Ask them if they think this is fair. I'm betting not a one of them will agree with you."

There was a hush over the crowd just before they all fell to their bellies and curled wings around themselves. Chase knew without looking that it was Emerald. They knew her, knew what she was capable of too. He turned to look at her, marveling at the beauty and poise of his mate. When he

147

started to step back, to let her take over, she shook her head.

"No, you're doing fine. I've only come to the meeting because I didn't know where you were. Go on, Chase. You've got this." He wasn't so sure, but didn't say it aloud. Instead he moved to stand next to her and held her hand. *If you back down, love, they'll never respect you.*

Chase turned back to the group as a whole. He knew that she was right, but to have a group of dragons, most of them bigger than he was, pissed off, Chase thought this a monumentally bad idea.

"Ask her what she thinks. I'm betting she tells you that you're not to do this again. I don't know why that speck went for you when the queen is right there." He glanced at Emerald, who looked as if she were looking at her nails. Turning back to the dragon, Chase smiled. Emerald was right. He had to do this now.

"I don't need to ask my mate what I need to do about you. I've made my decision, and I'm going to stand by it."

The dragon asked Emerald what she was going to do about him.

"I'm sorry, what did you ask me?" The dragon told her, from the beginning, of what had started this and how sorry he was. "And what was his punishment toward you? I'm sure that he did say one."

"Yes, he expected me to give up my things for money, and that I was to help them in some way of getting their building back in shape. I told him I was sorry, and that I'd never do it again, but he's on this power trip, and I don't like it. We both know that isn't going to happen. He's not going to destroy one such as me."

Emerald looked at Chase, then back at the dragon before speaking. "I'm not sure what you want me to say. I mean, did you want me to add to your punishment? Or perhaps destroy you now?" He said she wasn't listening to him. "Yes, I am. It is you who isn't listening. My mate, your king, has told you, in no uncertain terms, that you are to repay the people, make restitution for what you've done. Or, and this is the part that I love, he will destroy you. He's capable of it too. Just so you are aware of that." The dragon was nodding again, and Chase was sure he was trying the same thing he'd done to him on Emerald. "You have been warned before about this, haven't you?"

He waved her off. It was then that Chase had a chance to really look around. The others there, the ones that had come to see the show, they weren't happy either. Whether at him or the dragon, he wasn't sure, but he was nervous. Then one of them stood up, his face full of anger, and pointed to the dragon on the ground still.

"My lord. He has taken my moonstone flowers and seeds. He sells them, to other dragons, then steals them back. I should like to file a complaint against him." The dragon in question told him to shut up and sit down. He almost did, but stood again. "He is a terrible name for the dragons, my lord. I should like to be reimbursed as well. My moonstone seeds are of the highest quality, and even the queen of faeries has said so. I would like them returned and more so."

The next dragon stood up when seed dragon sat down. "This dragon has threatened me for many moons, my lord. Just last month, before coming here, he said that he was going to be king of us all, and that I was going to be his slave. He has demanded that I give him my flowers so that he does not have to work the gardens. I have a family, my lord. I don't have the extras that he is demanding of me. Should you destroy him now, I believe there will be more harmony with all of the rest of us. He is a terrible dragon."

"They're all just jealous." Chase asked him of what. "I am

149

a great dragon. I have been around for a very long time. And I don't have to do what others do."

"I think you have that all wrong. And you will do what the others do, as well as what I tell you, or die." The dragon looked at Emerald. "Don't look to her for guidance. I'm speaking now. If she had come here before me, I think you'd get off worse than you are now."

Emerald nodded and stood up. After kissing him on the cheek, she said she'd see him at the house. Then she asked Soto to stay in the event that he might need to learn how to destroy a dragon. When she was out of sight, Chase looked at the dragon.

"Do you agree to the punishment set before you?" The dragon looked around, then back at him. "I've asked you a question. I demand an answer."

The word demand...he'd known that it would have effects on the dragon, the same as it did on inferior or younger vampires. How much he had no idea, but it held a lot of force. Magic that would make a full-grown dragon whimper. Tears of blood, not gems, would fall from his eyes. When the dragon fell to the ground, crying out with pain, Chase watched him and said not a word.

"Yes. Yes, I'll do it. Take it back." He wasn't sure how to do that, but thought he didn't really want to take it back. Power...he needed to show them all that he was the one in charge and with the most power. Chase walked in the direction that Emerald had taken, with Soto telling him what a fine job he'd done the entire way.

Before he made it to the tree line, he knew that he was going to be sick. Even as he bent over behind the largest tree, he saw Emerald waiting. Puking up his dinner, Chase sat against the tree and tried to calm his nerves. He'd just stood up to a dragon and lived.

~~~

Harold wasn't sure where he had picked up the little bug that was forever in front of him. It spoke to him, telling him about her day, what she was used for, and when she went into hibernation. Which to him seemed a very long time, but he didn't speak to the faerie, what she called herself. The last time he had, she'd gotten him tossed out of the library when nobody but him could see or hear her. That was why he was sitting here, on the bench in front of it, trying to figure out what he had to do.

The computer that he'd been using in the library was free, but it had been old. Most of the people in there using them with him had been old too. But he needed to contact someone in his department to see when he was going to be reinstated. He had to get his job back. Harold was bored, and he had a great many things that he needed to do. Like find out about the woman and her supposed magical abilities. Not to mention, get his department back together once more.

He was no longer worried about the warrants out for his arrest. Harold was sure, once he talked to Lindsey, they'd be taken care of as well. But getting things done was much harder than he had anticipated. And much more complicated.

He knew that his men were all just sitting around, not doing anything. He'd seen it before. That was why he ran such a tight ship. Also, it was why, in the beginning, his teams had the record of having the most closed cases. Not anymore. People were lazy, he'd begun to see,. Lazy and not committed to anything but their stupid phones.

The faerie sat on his leg and he tried his best to ignore it.

"You know that the queen picked me alone to come and hang out with you. I wasn't sure what that term was, but after Lord Chase explained to me, I was very excited. Are you happy to be hanging out with me?" She paused in her speaking, and he could swear his ears sighed in relief, but it was short-lived. "You didn't answer me. Are you happy with being with me?"

"No, I am not. I wish for you to return to where you came from. Leave me alone. I don't even think that you're real." She grinned at him, her tiny little teeth sparkled in the morning light. "Go away. Shoo."

"Nay, I cannot. We are hanging together." He drew back his hand to swat at her again and she laughed. "You do that again and I will not be so nice to you the next time. You could have harmed me."

"That was the point." He put his hand down. If he was honest with himself, he was terrified of the little thing. She might be no bigger than his finger, but she surely did have a powerful punch to herself. "I wish to be left alone. And if you can't leave me alone, then stop talking all the time. I'm exhausted."

"You should sleep better. I noticed that every time that I woke you to ask you a question, you were very rude. Is it because you are not getting what you want?" Harold told her it was because she woke him all the time. "No, that cannot be it. I wake everyone every few hours. It is so that we can work. You will get used to my ways, then I will go to a normal schedule for you. Every hour you must be awakened to work for two. It is how we are able to get all the flowers ready for spring. I have been easy on you because you are not used to the way we do things."

"Why would I want to do things the way that you do?" She told him he was being silly again. He'd noticed that, when she didn't have an answer that he wanted to hear, she called him silly. Whatever that meant. "I would like to talk to the person who assigned you to me. To be waking me all the time, and who told you to annoy me. I want to talk to that person."

"She is the queen of the faeries. There is also the king and queen of the dragons. They have set me upon this task to make sure that you are going to be able to withstand the hours we have. It is such an honor for me to be with you all the time. You have no idea." He wanted to scream. And had he his gun, he thought he might well have shot her. There could not be a more annoying person in the world than her. "You must be very happy to be here with me. You have done nothing but talk-talk-talk to me. You'll see, when you are rested and on the faerie schedule, you'll be so much more productive."

"I want to take that woman, the one you call Emerald, back to my job so that she can tell them what she told me. That she is magical and has been around forever." She laughed and told him that wasn't going to happen. "Why not? I'm sure that there will be a lot of people who would like to get to know her, and what she can do. She'll be famous. Everyone likes to be celebrated. And I would be too. Famous, I mean."

"They will destroy her." He shook his head. "One of my kind, they were taken to a lab, such as the one you have in your mind. They tore off his wings and then put him in a dark cage. Faeries need light. All the time. Even when we are sleeping, we still like the lights. They cut him off from his light and he withered and died."

"That won't happen to her. I'll make sure of it." Harold needed this to happen. He'd say anything, promise whatever she wanted, to make sure that he got her to the building so that he could have his job back. "I need for her to cooperate. She's the only one that can fix this."

He noticed that people were staring at him. Again. Harold turned away from the faerie to look around. There were a lot of people around now, and some of them were actually pointing their phones at him. He had no doubt they were thinking him insane, but he did have a hope that one of them would be able to see the little person on his leg and speculate that was who he was conversing with.

And twice now, when he'd gone to have a meal, those men had come to join him. Well, join was overstated as to what they did. All they did was take his food then order more pie, and then foot him with the bill. He was tremendously tired of that as well.

"You are talking to no one again." She had pointed that out to him several times over the last few days. He glanced in her direction and said nothing. "You have a friend that I cannot see? I should like to meet them. Perhaps they could be my friend as well."

"I don't have a friend. And you're not my friend either. You're annoying. And a pain in my ass." He looked at her again. "Why did someone assign you to me? To drive me nuts? I think that's it. Well, it won't work. I'm smarter than that. I am not insane."

"I do not think that you are." She flittered—no other word for the way that she flew around his head—she flittered up to be in front of his face and smiled. "And I am too your friend. You may not think so, but you say my name in that tone all the time. I have asked, it means you are endeared to me."

"Who told you that? Emerald? The faerie queen? I'm betting that they have all kinds of sayings about how I feel about you." She smiled bigger, and he had to blink several times when the glint off her teeth hurt his eyes. "Why are you so shiny? Is it because of what you are, or are you covered in some kind of dust?"

He had no idea why he asked her that. She'd talk about it for hours now. But perhaps that was a good way for him to think. Having her prattle on about nothing might make it so he could tune her out.

154

"I have gems over my body. It is to make me shine better for the flowers. My shine is good, you see. When the sun hits me just right, the flowers can have more light. It is why some of us are covered in what you call diamonds." She went on about other gems, but it was what she had on her body that startled him. Diamonds? She was covered in diamonds. When he put out his hand for her to land on, he pulled her almost to his nose. "You wish to see me better?"

"Yes. I want to see how many diamonds are on you. I see none." She moved her wings then, and he could see how they gleamed, but no diamonds. Another bust, he thought. No one in their right mind would believe she had any on her if he were to tell them. Putting his hand on his lap, he decided he'd had enough of her for one day and stood up.

"I'm going to lie down for a bit. I do not want you to disturb me. I've a headache and I'd like to be alone." Of course she didn't leave, nor did she shut up. Harold had a feeling that he was going to be stuck with this thing all through his afterlife. If there was even that. He wasn't sure of a great many things any longer.

Chapter 13

The fields were ready for the coming spring. Chase noticed that his dragon, the one that he'd had to discipline, had been working, but not all that hard. He was going to have to take care of him soon. If not, then the others would come to him about his misdeeds again.

"The list, the one that I gave you days ago, do you still have it?" He looked at his brother Grayson and nodded. He'd been working with him all day, and it was the first time he'd spoken to him. He asked him what was wrong. "I have a lot on my mind right now. There is some major shit going on with the two companies that I have."

"I have nothing but time to help you with it if you want. Since we've hired a staff and a cook, I'm pretty much a free man a lot of the time." Grayson asked him about the dragons. "Just one is giving me a hard time, but soon enough, I think he's going to have to either pull his weight or be dealt with. I don't want to think about that right now."

"Yeah, I spoke to Emerald the other day. She said that you did a bang up job out in the field. I'm proud of you." He thanked him and wondered if he'd heard that he'd been so sick after that he'd had to lay down. And every time he thought of what he'd threatened a large dragon with, he had the shakes. "Maybe you can help me. It's the winery that we own. The one that also makes the labels as well?"

"Yes, you said that it would not only save you time in having them printed there, but also you could make changes without extra cost." Grayson nodded. "So, what can I help you with?"

"Three days ago, we got a shipment returned. There was, as far as I can tell, nothing wrong with it. And when I called the company, all I got was, they were going with another brand. I didn't think much of it until this morning, when I got a second call. This one said he was returning the wine and that he'd not be doing business with me again. I have a feeling that I know what it is, but I don't know who to call about it." He asked him to explain. "I think it's the Fed guy. I don't know why, but these people that are making the returns, they're hostile to me. Pissed off royally, but won't say why."

"Did you ask Jamie to look into it?" He said that he hadn't, he was worried the guy would get stressed again. "I can see that, but he won't. And if he were to get even a little bit stressed, I'd feel it and could calm him. I'll go with you, if you'd like."

"Yes, I'd very much like that. To be honest, while I don't need the income, it's one of those things that is nagging at me. And it's worrying the people that work there." Chase asked him what the second thing was. "That is more personal. And if I tell you, will you promise not to share it with anyone?"

"Of course." Grayson hopped into his truck while Chase got in the passenger side. "Do you need to show me something? Or are we headed to Jamie's place?"

"Both." He laughed. "Okay, I bought myself a bigger house. One that I'm anticipating a mate to come to me in.

With you and Jason having found yours, I figure it's only a matter of time before the rest of us do. I mean, Dad even found himself a second chance at love. While I'm not sure I know how to woo or love someone like a mate, I want to be as prepared as I can."

They drove to the other side of town and pulled up in front of a gated driveway. Once they were back in the truck after unlocking the gate, Chase noticed how much work was being done on the yards and trees. He commented on it as they drove up the snow-covered drive.

"It's big, the house, and there is a lot of acreage. About a thousand. I wanted big enough to expand, should I ever need to, and enough land that I didn't have to worry about neighbors. Not that I'm anti-social, I just like my privacy." As they rounded the trees that were bare right now, Chase got his first look at the house. Whistling, he looked over when Grayson laughed. "Yeah, that was my first reaction when I saw it too."

"This used to be the governor's house, didn't it?" Grayson said it had been, but it had fallen on hard times a while back. "I love the grand old entrance, Grayson, and the gables on the roof. This is beautiful."

"Yes, but it needs a lot of updating. That's where you can help me too. I cook, but maybe my mate will as well. Anyway, come inside, but watch your step, the floors are being replaced in places too." He and his brother entered the house, and all Chase could do was stare. It was in bad shape, but he could see the coming beauty in it too. "The window at the top of the stairs had all but been broken out. I'm having someone make a replacement, but more to my tastes. The one that had been in there before, I don't think it reflected anything but glass put together, if I remember correctly."

They had come here, decades ago, when the house had

been new. There had been no electricity in the house, not even a bathroom back then. But even then, it had been a spectacular place. Grand. As they made their way to the kitchen, where it looked as if the most work was being done right now, he could see why Grayson needed help.

"It's too small. And you need a pantry too." Grayson pulled out his tablet and started writing things down on it. "I'd take out the windows here and put in a single large one. These tiny ones are not going to let in much light."

"I thought that too, but I didn't know if it stemmed from me loving the outdoors or simply that's what it needed." Grayson walked out the kitchen door that seemed to go right into another building. This door was thick, solid, and covered on the inside with hooks, which were all around the room. "This is a building I have no idea what it might have been used for. I thought a smokehouse, but there isn't that sort of smell to it. You know, woodsy. And these strange hooks? What do you suppose they might have held?"

Chase walked to them and had no idea either, but when he reached up to touch one of them, a flood of information and images flashed though his mind. Once he was able to let the hook go, he staggered a little then fell to the floor. It took him several minutes to answer his brother as he was saying his name.

"I'm all right. I just…. I know what they were used for. And trust me when I tell you, you need to take them out. In fact, this entire building needs to go." Grayson said that he would, but needed to know what he saw. "This place was for the slaves. They would be hung here, sometimes for days at a time, and the cook would come in and throw the slop jars on them. The thickness of the doors was to keep out the smell as well as any noises that were made. Christ, Grayson, this building was put here just for that. Close enough to beat them, and they could smell the food coming from the kitchen while they starved out here."

"It's coming down. Today." Chase nodded and let Grayson help him stand up. "How did you see that, if you don't mind me asking?"

"I have no idea. More stuff from Emerald, perhaps? I don't know. I'll see what I can find out from her when I see her the next time." He would too. While this sort of thing might be helpful, a little heads up would keep him from touching something that he shouldn't.

They went through the rest of the house, but now, Chase was careful not to touch anything. He didn't want to see what the rooms might hold. What some of the pieces of furniture might tell him. As soon as they were back to the truck, Chase saw that the building as well as a part of the kitchen was already torn out. He'd bet anything by this time tomorrow, not only would no one know there had been that building, but the windows for the kitchen would be ready to install.

Their next stop was at the Nash home. Jamie was in the kitchen with Kristie, and they were having a nice lunch. Kristie insisted they join them, and both him and his brother were handed a large sub as well as a glass of tea. Chase was halfway through his while Grayson told Jamie what was going on.

"That sounds like something that Bates would do. Let me make a few calls and I'll let you know." Jamie got up and left them there, and Grayson told Kristie he was sorry. He'd not meant now.

"You have no idea how bored he is right now. Last night, I caught him going through seed catalogs. And he's talking about getting a small tractor to use. I think he really wants to work with his hands, but since he can't do much more than dream of this garden project because of the time of year, he's

KATHI S. BARTON

trying to find things to keep his mind going." Chase asked her if Jamie was really going to be a house husband. "Yes, though not all the time, but most of it. He said that he might need adult contact after a while, but he wants to be there for our child."

"I think it's wonderful." Neither he nor Emerald had told anyone that she was breeding. He hadn't been sure that anyone else, like his brothers, might know, but they didn't seem to. "How are you liking the new doctor?"

"I love her. She's a hoot. But I'm glad that you're here today. I have a problem with my last check, and the two other checks that I got." Chase asked her what it was. "Well, it's double, for one thing. Then I have a check for a vehicle that I need to purchase. And the third check is for a building. I went to look yesterday. I thought it was a typo, that it was for an office, but apparently, I'm to purchase this entire building and have it in my name. Why are you guys doing this?"

"The family is, yes. And there are two reasons. One, we like you, and expect you to do great things for both us and the pack that you're working with. Secondly, we like you." She pointed out that he'd said that already. "Well, it bears repeating. As for the increase in your pay, we realized that we were only paying you standard for being a company attorney, but you're far more than that. You're being an attorney for our family and businesses, as well as the pack. That is double duty on your part."

"It's really not, and both are very easy to do." Grayson laughed. "Why is that funny?"

"You have no idea what sort of trouble we get into all the time." He smiled at her when she looked at him. Grayson wasn't telling her the whole truth, but in this, he thought it was a good idea to let her think she was going to be very busy. "Besides, you're learning a lot of law that you'd never

162

find in books at college. You will need it in the coming years, and we're thrilled that you can do it for us."

Jamie joined them again, but he looked perplexed. When Grayson asked him what he'd found out, he said that he needed one more phone call to come in. And once that was in, he'd be able to tell him. The phone rang in that minute and he answered it. As he spoke to the person on the other end, Chase got nervous.

~~~

Jamie hung up and stood there. This was the strangest thing he'd ever dealt with. So, when he sat down again, he looked at the two men with him. One he owed his very life to, the other had become a good friend as well.

"Bates, as you might have guessed. I had no idea that he could.... Well, what he's done is put it out there that you're under investigation. For what, no one seems to know. But after I got the last call, it became clear for all of us. He told them to look into you for being an alien. Not like from another country, but a different realm." Grayson laughed, and so did Chase. It was funny, he supposed, but also a little frightening for him. "He is telling his people, the ones that worked for him, to cut all ties you have with everyone. I'm not sure why your business was the first one, but it's been taken care of now. My buddy at the offices, he's putting it out there that not only were you helping the government with some projects that have to do with bee pollination, but also their effects on winery. A lot, I'm told."

"Yes, bees are extremely helpful to all plant life. So, he's had this notion put out there so that I'd be in trouble. Now what?" Jamie told Grayson that it was done. That no more would be said about it. "So that's it? Everything will be fine now?"

"No. I have a feeling that since you've been put out there

163

as a man with a mission, helping the planet, you might see an increase in business. At least that's what my buddy told me. He's going to make sure of it." Grayson laughed again, and Jamie felt better. "You're not mad?"

"No. I mean, I might have been had it worked for Bates, but no, I'm not mad. What good would that do?" Jamie nodded, wishing that he could be more like these men, taking things in stride and not getting upset when it didn't go his way. "Now, I need you for something. No biggie, but it's going to help us both. What do you know about gardening?"

"Nothing. I'm guessing that Kristie told you I was bored. I am, but you don't have to make up work for me." Grayson assured him that he wasn't. "Then I'll help you in any way that I can."

Grayson told him what he needed, what the dragons needed, and where the new gardens were being put in. It sounded like a huge undertaking, but he was game for anything that got him out of the house for a few hours and gave him some way to work his head. He really wasn't used to being idle so much.

"I can do that. I mean, I'd have to learn, of course, but I can help with the planning." He was to organize and make sure that the faeries were having plants coming on at different times of the year. Not all just in the spring. "I've been reading up on plants for this region. There are a great many of them that we can work with."

"That is something else. The land that is closest to and on the faerie land can be planted year-round. It's not really all that big, but they use it for things like starters, as well as trees that they're trying to cross pollinate." Jamie stared taking notes, something that he did all the time, but now it was fun looking them over when he put them in his computer. "I love to read, so I have a lot of books on a great many subjects, but

I can recall things better than most computers, I think. So, if you have any questions about this or any of the projects, all you need to do is ask. I'm sure that if I don't know the answer, someone will be able to help us."

When the two of them left, Jamie sat down at his computer again and started making lists. All the plants that he'd wanted to put into his own garden were still there, but the second list he made was for timing. There was an art to it, he'd seen, so that gardens, flower or otherwise, would be blooming year-round, as they wanted to happen.

By the time Kristie came to remind him to come up for air, something that she'd done when he'd been working for the government, he stood up and danced with her around the room. She started laughing, and Jamie realized how much he'd missed that from her. Just the simple sound of her laughter.

"If you're in this good of a mood just because you get to play in the dirt, you're going to love this. I just got a call from Elliot. He has a home in France that I need to go see to make sure that its repairs are being done. And if not, then I'm to make it happen." He asked her if he could go. "Of course. Elliot said that we should scope out the other houses around, to make sure that there wasn't anything for sale that he might like to purchase, and I'm to bring home things, on their credit card, that might be a nice addition to the shops here in town. Oh, Jamie, this is going to be fun, working for these men."

He had had it in his head that they'd be making up work for him to do. Something easy that would keep him working and paid, but not too difficult. Not that going to France or making lists was hard, but he could see the real value in it. The reasons that these men were very wealthy...they did nothing half-assed. Nor did they spare expenses when things were needing repairs.

"We should be gone a week, he told me. And while gone,

they'll have someone come in and keep the house for us. Cleaning and watering the plants." Jamie nodded, already thinking of things that he'd like to do while in France with his lovely wife. "He said that there are tickets for shows, too, that we might as well use. I looked into it, Jamie. There really are tickets that they don't use, and usually end up donating them to someone else to go. This job is going to be epic if this keeps up."

Today was Wednesday and they were leaving on Monday. A lot of planning needed to be done and things arranged. Not only was he having the nursery set up, but now he could get it done without her knowing. Making a mental note to call one of the brothers to help him out with it, he was excited to have this happening when it did.

"You know, I asked him about the baby and how we would travel after it's born. He said that I wasn't to worry about it, that I'd have more than enough babysitters should we need them. Not to mention, the trips would all be baby friendly, as well as a nanny would be with us to help with the extra work. These men really know how to treat someone."

"I agree. And the fact that I'm going to be working for such a big project, I've never felt so good in my life, honey. I mean, yes, it's stressful, but in a fun, I'm enjoying this too much to have a heart attack sort of stress." She told him he'd better never have another heart attack. "I won't. I promise you. I mean, I'll promise you that I won't let myself be that stressed again."

"I can live with that. We have a child to raise, and we're going to raise it together. I don't want to be alone doing this, Jamie. I need you here." He nodded and held her, feeling the baby kick him as he held his momma. "I love you, with all that I am."

"And I love you. Now, what do we need to get going on

this job of yours?" They were laughing as they made their way to the bedroom to see what they would need to take or buy.

Jamie had yet to tell her that they were both going to live forever. Chase had told him only the other day, and he was trying to think of a way to break it to his lovely wife. Their children would be around as well. And while Jamie was sure she'd not be mad about it, he just didn't know. And that was what was keeping him from telling her.

But perhaps this trip would be the perfect time. She'd be happy, and so would he. He thought about buying her something pretty while there, and wondered if any of the Crosby men knew of a place he could get his pretty wife a gift for simply loving him. He was sure they'd know…they were men that had a good knowledge of a great many things, he'd come to find out.

Chapter 14

Elliot walked up and down the new aisles he'd put in today. They were straight and long, much better than the original ones he'd had put in a decade ago. Crosby Flowers was doing a much better business than he'd ever dreamed it would, and he was planning to hire six more people this year to help with the planting.

He had a strange business for a vampire. Elliot knew this, but it was fun for him too. People, humans especially, would never guess that he was a night walker. Sometimes even he had trouble remembering he was. As he set up the water system, Elliot thought of all the things he'd done in his lifetime. Most of it had been outdoor jobs, but there had been a few that had kept him in a building.

For a while he'd been a grave digger. It had only paid the bills, as far as he was concerned. There was nothing, not one thing else, that he could think that was good about the job. He had hated it more than he did himself back then.

Then he'd been a surgeon. That hadn't been a smart choice for him. He was good at it, very good, but when one of his patients would pass over, he'd go into a deep depression that would last for several days. He'd gotten out of that line of work in about ten years.

Elliot knew that in order to have the plants ready for spring planting, he had to work most of the colder months. November would be for set up. Since he didn't have to do it all on his own this year, he was actually thinking of waiting until December. Then the rest of that month into early March, they were not just planting herbs for the spring plant, but also long-term things. Tomatoes for one thing. Then there were flowers that would be ready for Memorial Day.

The water started flowing in the direction that he needed it to. As soon as he didn't see any leaks, he turned it off. Just as he was turning to see to the other lines, he saw the little boy in the corner, his coat almost the same color as the gray walls he was near. Instead of scaring him, Elliot continued working on his lines.

When he was finished with all of them, he pulled out his lunch. He hadn't really planned on eating it. There was a perfectly good cold pizza at home that he had planned on having for dinner, but the kid was hungry. Even from the distance across the room, Elliot could hear his belly growling.

"I have two sandwiches here if you want one." The kid didn't move, so he opened the bottle of water he had as well. "There is a roast beef one with tomatoes on it, as well as a turkey and bacon one. Which do you want?"

The kid came out of the corner, but he didn't move any closer. Elliot knew that he was afraid of him. So, he not only didn't make any sudden moves, but told him what he was going to do next. As he pulled out the napkins that were also in his bag, the kid took a few steps toward him.

"You're a vampire." Elliot said that he was. "I don't know how you're in here when you're that. The sun has been shining for a long time."

"I have a special power. Do you want one of these?" He nodded, but didn't move. "If you want one of them, you're going to have to come and get it. I won't wait on you hand and foot."

The kid moved to the little table, but didn't reach for the sandwich or the offered bottle of water. Instead, Elliot cut the two sandwiches in half and bit into the roast beef one.

"My momma is dead." The kid sat down and took the other half of the beef sandwich. "She'd been real sick, and my dad, he's not happy with me."

"Why is that?" He gave him the bottle of water and wished that he had something like juice for him. "Is he upset with you, or the fact that your momma died?"

"I don't know. He's always mad, I think."

Elliot reached out gently and read the boys mind. The kid was abused. A great deal, and had been staying in the green house for several days now, hiding from his dad.

"Are you gonna tell him that I'm here?"

There was more there too. Like the fact that the mother hadn't just died, but had been killed. And no one, not a person of authority, knew about it. She was under the porch, wrapped up in a plastic tarp.

"No, not if you don't want me to." And he wouldn't either. If the police asked him, which he doubted anyone would come to him about a missing kid, then he'd have to. But for now, the kid could stay here as long as he wanted. "I'll make sure that you have food here. Nothing to cook, I'm afraid. The microwave took a dump a few weeks ago."

"I don't mind cold stuff. I hope you don't care, but I had your candy bar for breakfast." Elliot would make sure that there was less candy in his desk and more good snacks from now on. "This is really good. Did your momma make it for you?"

171

"No, my mom is gone as well. She died when I was younger." The kid nodded but said nothing as he ate the other two halves of sandwiches. "What's your name? I don't need your last, but I have to have something besides '*kid*' to call you."

"Dad calls me shit for brains. I don't want you to call me that, okay?" Elliot said he didn't want to call him that either. "My real name is Cody. I'm nine."

"My name is Elliot Crosby." The kid polished off the sandwiches and was looking around the room. "I have a cot in the office that you can use. There's a telephone in there as well. I'm going to write down my phone number, and you can call me when you need to."

"You gonna eat me? I know that you said you was a vampire and all, but you ate a sandwich. Are you gonna make me pay you back with my neck?" Elliot told him he didn't feed from friends. "Am I your friend then, Mr. Crosby?"

"Yes, so long as you don't hurt anything in here, we'll be just fine." He knew on some level that he should tell someone that the boy was in here. But he also knew that the kid trusted less than he did, and that was saying a lot. "Also, there will be food in here. And water. You eat what you want, and I'll replace it. Does anyone else know that you're here?"

"No. Just you. Did you know that there are kids that come around here at night and try to get in?" He said that he didn't, but he'd make sure they couldn't get in. "Thanks. You're not going to hurt them, are you? I think they're just having fun."

"I'm not a terrible person, Cody. Just a man that has a business. Who just happens to be a vampire." Cody nodded and played around with the water circles on the table. "You want a job? I'll pay you. I need someone to make sure that the heat stays on in here at night. I'm worried that if it gets too cold, the pipes will burst, and I'll have to start over again."

"I can do that. It's nice and warm in here now." Elliot told him that he was warming it up to get the soil ready for planting. "That's a good idea. I'd sure hate to have all those pretty plants die that my momma liked to look at."

Cody made his way to the office, and Elliot gently reached out to see what sort of injuries had been done to the young man. Plenty. Some of them old, but a lot of fresh wounds too. He was going to have to figure out who his father was and where he lived, to make sure the man understood the precious gift he'd been given.

Elliot showed him the office and helped him make up the little cot. It had been in the place when he'd bought it, and he'd had no reason to use it. Not only did it have a couple of worn out blankets, but a nearly flat pillow too. Cody acted like he'd given him the keys to the toy store, he was so happy.

After making sure that the kid was going to be all right, Elliot made his way to the store. There was a nice fridge in the place, but he wanted to make sure that Cody had something more to eat than just cold food. Buying a microwave along with the food, he was checking out the produce when he saw a pack member, Libby, standing in front of the deli. Going to her, he asked if she was all right.

"I.... Yes. I was just thinking about this man that was in the parking lot when I came in. He gave me the creeps." Elliot asked her in what way. "I don't know. It wasn't like he'd done anything to me. Or even said anything other than asking me about his little boy and a dog, but I had the feeling that there was more to it than that."

Elliot decided to trust her with his secret, and she asked him if the little boy needed to be in a home. He told her that he had no idea, but that he was terrified of his father and that he was keeping him safe for now. She looked at his cart and his face heated up.

173

KATHI S. BARTON

"Yeah, so I'm making sure he has food too. I didn't see a dog, but that doesn't mean there wasn't one with him. Do you suppose I should get some treats for him too?" She laughed and told him that half the stuff in his cart wasn't going to cut it either. "It has been a long time since I was a little boy, you know."

"I would imagine that you didn't have a lot of occasion to have a meal then, either." They both laughed, and she helped him purchase things that she thought Cody would eat. "Give him my number as well, will you? I mean, I know that you'd help him if he called, but sometimes he might need a mom figure. I don't know why. I mean, he has lost his mom, so maybe he might need a female to talk to."

"I'll do that. I'll tell him that you're my step-mom, and that I trust you not to tell on him." Libby thanked him, and he asked her if she was all right now.

"I am. I was just.... It makes me feel better to know that Cody isn't running around in the cold. But that man, I don't know what it was about him, but I don't want Cody to go back there. He isn't right." Elliot said he'd make sure that he was safe and left the store.

After putting the groceries away, he handed Cody the cell phone that he'd picked up too. Telling him that if he had to run, that he should call him immediately and he'd come for him. It was a chance he was taking, harboring a little boy from his father, but it was something he was willing to do. Then he asked about the dog.

"His name is Buster. I had to leave him outside because I can't take him out to poop without my dad seeing me." He told him that he'd be fine now, only not to go beyond the parking lot. "You can make us safe that way too?"

"Yes, I can, but you have to remember, don't go beyond the parking lot. Okay?" Cody assured him that he wouldn't

174

and the little pup, a mutt actually, was brought inside. "I'll make sure that he's all right tomorrow. I have a friend that is a vet. And my friend Libby, she said to call her if you need someone to talk to."

After going home, Elliot sat with his phone on his lap for the rest of the night, hoping that Cody would call him, and hoping he didn't have to. It was a scary thing, being responsible for a kid, he thought.

~~~

Emerald called Agent Lindsey at noon, knowing that it was high time that someone collected Mr. Bates. She told the man that he'd been noticed around town talking to himself, as well as making calls to local businesses to tell them that she was magical.

"I don't know why he has this obsession with me. Every time I see him on the streets, he comes after me, threatening me about talking to his boss. Today when I saw him, he handed me this number and said that I should call you. To tell you that he needs his job back." Bates hadn't, but she had gotten Lindsey's number from him. "I just don't know what to do, Agent Lindsey. It's getting to the point where I'm afraid to go into town alone."

She wasn't afraid at all. In fact, she made it a point to seek the man out whenever she could. And when there were others around, witnesses, she provoked Bates into a debate about how magical she was. It was fun really, but things were wearing thin and she needed him safe.

"I will be on the next plane to talk to him. I was there until recently, but family troubles brought me home. I'm so sorry about this. I swear to you, Mrs. Crosby, I'll make sure that no harm comes to you." She thought of the harm that could come of Bates if he kept at this. "I'm very sorry about this. I had no idea that he'd gone this far in this. His employee, Agent Nash,

175

he's in your area too, isn't he?"

"Yes. I've become good friends with his wife. She's expecting a baby soon. They're getting along nicely, I think, but Jamie has to take it easy now. Poor man. To have had such trouble for someone so young." He told her that he would visit him as well. "I think he'd like that. Mr. Bates; he's been harassing Kristie too, if you can believe that. He's becoming a problem, Agent Lindsey, and I'm worried that he'll be harmed."

"Yes, you leave it to me and I'll come and see to him." He put her on hold, and Chase asked her when she'd gotten so sickly sweet all of a sudden. Before she could tell him to fuck off, Lindsey was back on the line. "I'll be there in the morning. First thing. We'll get this taken care of. I promise."

When she hung up the phone, she sat down at the table with Chase. He had told her what he'd thought of the man, Bates, and what he'd seen him doing today. There were several complaints about his language too, he'd told her. And he was scaring the kids at the library as well.

"Sandy has been with him for several days now, and she said that he's really having a hard time of it. I guess she wakes him every hour on the dot to get him up and moving. It's playing with his mind." Chase asked her why she'd do that. "It's the faerie schedule. They rest for an hour and work two. It's the only way they can get all the flowers ready for spring. She was picked because she is never one to be quiet."

"I heard Bates telling her a few times to shut up. But he never hurts her. I guess he did try once, but that didn't go over too well." Emerald said she'd bet not. "Also, she's having fun, too, from what Kilian says. When she reports to her on his actions, Kilian said it's all she can do sometimes not to have her go back and get on his nerves more."

"Well, we'll have to see what tomorrow brings. I'm

betting that once he's in a room with him, Lindsey will have no choice but to have him committed. And that would be the safest place for him. I've been doing some walking through his mind. And while he's not hurt anyone physically, he has been involved in quite a few incidences where mentally, there was a problem. And what he did to Jamie too."

Emerald looked over the chart that Jamie had given her before he left. It was the planting schedule that he'd been asked to make up. At the rate that he had the faeries and other creatures planting and harvesting, they'd be busy all spring and well into winter. He even had them planting wheat for the birds to eat for the colder months. She showed it to Chase.

"He's been reading up on plants for some time now, I guess." He looked at the chart and then handed it back to her. "I wonder what else he could apply this sort of planning to. I mean, can you imagine the schedules he could make for just about anything once he sets his mind to it?"

"That's what I was thinking when I saw it. Plants are complicated, I think. Different seasons, with various lengths to produce. What if he applied this knowledge to the plant that Jewel has?" Chase asked her what she meant. "Well, there are a lot of people that cannot, for whatever reasons, work full time. Or even a full day. What if he got with their schedules and made it so that her plant was open every day and all day? She has enough orders, I heard, that she might need to open a second plant in another city, for more workers. If she were to be able to run this one all the time, she could keep the people in town working and everyone happy with their shifts."

"I love that idea."

They sat and talked about it for several hours. Emerald had a list of things that he could use his knowledge about charts on. Also, and this was exciting, there was the winery that they owned. "Grapes have a long growing life, and then a short time to pick them. If we could get the most out of the season, then the grapes could be used better instead of just picking what we can."

Emerald wasn't really sure how that worked. It was one of the few jobs that she'd never done. It had been something that was fought over, a great deal as a matter of fact, but she had little to do with the actual production of wine.

As they were setting up a time to go and talk to Jamie about his part in all this, Chase's phone rang. She started to leave him to his business when he asked her to stay. Agent Lindsey was still coming tomorrow, but he wanted them there when he spoke to Bates. Emerald thought that a wonderful idea.

Chapter 15

Harold wasn't sure what was going on with all the cameras and people in the room with them, but so long as he was given the opportunity to clear this mess up, he was all for anything that they wanted. He really needed his job back, and Harold figured this was the only way to do it.

Harold had seen his boss on the sidewalk earlier that morning. They talked for a bit, and then he was asked to meet him here at his hotel. Well, here he was, and there was no sign of either Lindsey or anyone else that he had asked to be here. When the door opened, just as he was ready to get out of there, in walked not just Nash, but that fat wife of his.

"What are you doing here? Shouldn't you be out watching for that woman? You are the laziest agent I have ever had the misfortune of having work for me. Get back to work. And don't think I won't remember his when I'm back to work myself." The pesky faerie told him to hush and he looked at her. "I will not hush up. I have things to say, and I'll not have you telling me that I should be quiet."

The camera men stopped moving, and they looked at him while he spoke to the bug. There was a smallish camera

179

pointed at him, and he was reasonably sure that it wasn't just a camera, but a video recorder as well. Harold asked him if he had permission to record him.

"Yes, sir. I do. When you signed on with the Bureau, you signed off on such things. It's only when you're out in the public eye that you can't have people doing this sort of thing." Harold asked him why he was doing it now. "I was told to set it up, and that's what I'm doing."

"You should smile at the camera. Not that one you give to me, but the nice one, the one that you save for when you're in a good mood." Harold glared at the faerie. "Well, do you want them to think you to be an ugly man?"

"I'm not an ugly man. I'm a good man with a good head on my shoulders. It's that fool over there that everyone should be worrying about." He pointed at Nash. "And why is his wife here? What could a woman add to this conversation? Nothing, I tell you, not one thing. I think I should leave."

"You leave, and they will come and find you. No. This is much better. You can speak to them all you wish. I will help you get the words straight so that you don't look the fool. You do not want them to think you foolish, do you?" Harold wasn't so sure she was going to be helpful, but decided that the sooner he got this over with, the faster he could get back to his job. "Now, sit up straight in your chair and try not to look mean."

He wanted to tell her that he was no such thing, but Nash and his fat wife were joined by the woman. Emerald, he'd been told her name was, and she looked so much prettier every time he saw her. But it was the man that she was with that had him protecting his balls. For some reason, the man gave off the feeling that he was sizing him up for his next meal. Whatever that might mean.

Judge Merkle showed up just as he was going to approach

the woman. He thought of using her name, but it wasn't real, so he figured that it would do him no good to show her that he had taken the time to find it out. Besides, he had a feeling that after today, she'd think she was gone from his life, and he could easily move on to more important things that would come his way. And there would be too.

"We're here to talk to one former agent, Harold Bates." He injected that he was going to be an agent again. "We'll have to see about that, now won't we? There are charges against you, Mr. Bates, that I have brought up to you before. And now we're going to add on your escaping from custody, as well as harassing the Crosby family."

"I don't even know who that is. You can't just add things onto me without having proof." The woman, Emerald, stood up and said that he was harassing her. "Yes, well, that's different. You're going to have to tell these people what you told me. And show them the dragon and man changing into a wolf. Show them. And tell them how you've been around a long time. I have pictures of her from the early eighteen hundreds, and she doesn't look a day older now than she did then."

"That, I can tell you, would be a relative of mine. As you know, Your Honor, people do not live forever." The stupid judge only nodded, and Harold had a feeling he was being bamboozled. Again. "As for the rest of his accusations, I don't know what he's talking about."

He looked down at the little faerie as he continued. "You were there. Tell them what you saw. Go on. You might have to get closer to her for her to hear you, but go on, tell them." The little thing just stared at him, then looked at the judge. "I know that she's a woman and all, but you have to make her believe that what I'm saying is true."

"Mr. Bates, who are you talking to?" The judge asked him

181

to behave himself. "I'll not have you making a mockery of these proceedings."

"Mockery? Don't you think you sitting up there is the biggest mockery there is? A woman pretending to be this judge? I'll have you know that in my time, women were to stay at home, raise the family up and make sure they knew the difference between right and wrong. Have you looked out into the world? Seen what a mess it is? And all because a few of you rabbles thought you were better than a man. No, you are not, young lady. You need to quit this right now and get back to where you belong. Serving a man in his castle. Having babies that are smart, and know the difference between right and wrong."

"Be that as it may, sir, you're the one on trial here, not me. I've come here with the understanding that you were going to be cooperative in getting this trouble you've started over with. I can see now that you aren't going to be any more helpful than you were before." He knew she was mad, it was written all over her face. But he didn't care right now. Things were not going to go his way until someone spoke up for him. And the faerie wasn't helping.

"You have to talk to her. She thinks she can get by with this, and now I'm going to be out on the streets if you don't." She told him that he wasn't helping himself by being mean again. "I'm not being mean, damn it. I'm trying to save my job."

"You don't need to work, sir. You just need to make them see that you're a nice man." She flew up to his chest and tsked at him. "Your tie is all askew. Straighten it up and you'll look better. I swear, I need to have two of me just to keep you looking good."

He fixed his tie and asked her if it was all right. Harold hadn't had a lot of time to spruce himself up. Plus, the water in his hotel room, the hovel, wasn't up to par, and he'd had to forego a shower and had done a spit bath. Nasty name for washing yourself up, but that's what he'd done. And now he was being told his tie was off.

Harold looked around the room when he asked her if his tie was all right. They were staring at him again, as if he were a bug under a microscope. When he asked what was wrong, none of them would look him in the eyes. It was as if they were embarrassed, for him.

"I've a few things to say." The faerie that had been his only companion for the last several days told him to be nice. "I am nice, damn it. Why must you keep telling me that? I'm just going to tell them what I've been telling you. That this woman needs to be taken in and studied."

"I've told you before, sir, that they'll harm her. And perhaps even kill her. There are beings out there that care not for how special she is to us. They'll only want to do their tests and make her into something less than she is." Harold told her that he'd not let that happen. "You won't have any way to stop it. They'll see that their way is the only way, much like you do, and they'll do as they please."

He told her that he'd make sure. It wasn't a promise that he knew that he could keep, and he was reasonably sure that the little bug knew it. But looking at the faces of the people in the room with him, he realized that they might know it as well. The woman, Emerald, was grinning at him. And he thought of all the things she'd said and done to him.

"She's the bad guy here. Her and her magical ways. Did you know that she claims to be the queen of dragons? That the man there beside her, he's the king? I've not met him as yet, but that's what I've been told." Lindsey asked him who had told him. "This faerie. She looks like a bug with shiny teeth, but she never stops talking. She tells me a great many

183

things, but that's beside the point. I need for you to believe me when I tell you that this woman isn't what she's pretending to be. And if Nash would have done his job instead of just taking up air space, then you'd all know it as well."

"Mr. Bates, there is no one there." He looked at the faerie, then back at Lindsey. "I don't know who you think you might be speaking to, but there is no faerie there, nor is there such a thing as dragons. Much less a king and queen of them. Are you feeling all right?"

"Yes, of course I am. I'm perfectly fine. I tell you, she's the one that is controlling them." Harold stood up. "You're not listening to me because she's put some sort of spell over you all. Not the faerie, of course, but the rest of you people."

It occurred to him then that he was being made to look like a fool. Or worse yet, a crazy man. Harold tried to think why they'd think that, and all he could come up with was the woman again. She was making it so that his job was in jeopardy. Worse than that, his sanity was in question. He sat down then and let out a long breath. He needed to regroup and to think. And he knew that he wasn't going to be able to do it here. Not with these people.

"I should like to reschedule this. I've a headache and I need to rest. I don't think that you're listening to me. And I don't like that that woman is here either. I'll come back some other time, when I have more proof of what she is." He stood again, and the men with guns that had been sliding in the room without his notice until now put their hands on their weapons. "You're going to shoot me? For what? I've done not one thing wrong. I'm coming back, just not with her here."

"You're not leaving here, Mr. Bates." He told the judge that he was Agent Bates. "No, you are not. Now, Mr. Bates, let's start again. What has Mrs. Crosby done to you that you feel you have to harass her?"

~~~

Bates was holding to his claim that Emerald Crosby was a queen of dragons, and that her husband was the king. There were other claims that he had, but the thing that bothered Paddy Lindsey the most was the way he kept having a conversation with his hand.

Well, it wasn't his hand, not what Bates was saying, but a faerie. A tiny one too, that he'd described in great detail, several times now. And she, this faerie, had also told him, that he needed to take a breath and let it out slowly, which he did. Paddy was sure that poor Bates was off his noodle. In more ways than one.

He was a mess. His hair looked as if he'd combed it with cacti. He'd not shaved in what appeared to be days. And his clothing was dirty, like he'd slept in it as well. The man he'd known was gone, and in his place was a disheveled shell of a person.

The questions that were being put to him were ones that he himself had written out. The judge, Lynn Merkle, had agreed to be an impartial judge on behalf of Bates. But even that wasn't going well. Everyone, including the men that he'd had come in to run the equipment, were shocked at some of his answers.

"Mr. Bates, what can you tell me about your leaving the hospital?" Bates asked her what she'd meant. "You were arrested, then taken to the hospital. What happened that made you want to leave the care given to you then?"

"I didn't want to be there." He looked down at his hand again. "The faerie said to tell you that you need to stop asking me this question. It's making me look bad."

"We're not here to make you look good or bad, Mr. Bates. We're here to get answers to a lot of questions. Some of them you've avoided. So, we'll try this one. Why did you

185

send Agent Nash here to find out what he could about Mrs. Crosby?"

"She wasn't Mrs. Crosby when I sent him to find her. And I didn't send him here. I just told him to find her. And to bring her in. He couldn't even do that part. I'm betting that his fat wife did that too. She's an evil one, that one is. And why does he get to be agent when I don't? I think he should be fired for dereliction of duty." She asked him what duty had he not done. "Find this woman, as I have told you several times before. Ten, as the faerie has been keeping count."

This was what he'd been hoping for, and not hoping he'd admit. Several times while he'd been employed by the agency, he'd been told not to pursue looking for this woman. And he'd done it, assigning a new person to the job, putting him away in the building so that no one would know about it, and continued on as if he'd not been warned. Standing up, Paddy looked at Bates with sadness.

"You continued to have Agent Nash search for this woman, when I had told you several times that you were to stop wasting tax payers' money on this." Bates told him he'd been wrong to do that. "So, you admit that you were warned. Yet you assigned an agent to continue working on the case anyway."

"Yes, and I'd do it again too. Don't you get it? She's acting like there isn't anything different about her, when we all know that she's not human. Shoot her. Go ahead and try and kill her. See that what I've been telling you is right." Paddy was shocked at the request. "Well, if you don't want to do it, then give me your gun and I'll do it. You'll see that she can't die. She told me that."

"Bates, what the fuck is wrong with you? You cannot kill a woman just because you think she might be an immortal. Things are not done that way." Again, Bates waved him off.

"You can't be serious. You actually think that one of us should fire at this woman to prove if your theory is correct?"

"Yes. I don't know why you're so squeamish about this, Lindsey. I mean, she told me straight out that she wasn't able to die. And you won't believe me any other way. So, shoot her. You'll see." He stood up and put out his hand, and Paddy looked at it then at Bates again. "Just hand me your weapon, Lindsey, and I'll show you. There are enough recording things going on around here that no one will blame you for it if I should be wrong, but I'm not. She's not going to be harmed at all. You'll see."

"You keep saying that." Paddy looked at Emerald. She was being held by her husband, and it broke Paddy's heart that the woman seemed to be sobbing. Her husband was glaring at Bates as if he might well do the man harm. This was nuts, more so than he thought Bates was now. "I think we've heard enough. Harold Bates has clearly lost his ability to have clear thought."

"Yes, I have to agree with you on that one." Judge Merkle just shook her head as she continued. "It gives me no pleasure in having to say this, but Mr. Harold Bates, I remand you over to a place where you can be tested for your mental capabilities. Until such time, you will be watched over so that no harm can come to you or others. These proceedings are closed."

Before much more time passed, Bates was handcuffed and taken out of the room. The judge stood up as well, and came to sit next to Paddy as she spoke to him in a quiet and sad voice.

"I'm sorry about this, Paddy. He's gotten a little worse since he was in my courtroom, and I'm sorry for that. Was he a good agent?" Paddy nodded. "Then I'm doubly sorry for this. But he didn't leave us much in the way of choice."

"Yes, in his time, he was even a likable man. But like a

lot of people, he'd gotten stuck in his job duties and what his power was. Not to mention, he sort of stuck himself in the fifties and never moved forward." Merkle laughed and said she got that too. "I'm sorry about that. I truly am."

"It's all right. He'll get some care now." He hoped so. Paddy surely hoped that he got a great deal of care now. "The tapes; if you don't mind, I'd like to have a transcript of them. Just for my own records."

"I'll ask." He knew as surely as he was sitting there that there would never be any transcripts of this proceeding, so that she could not read them over. As far as anyone would be concerned, this had never happened. And Bates, for all his insanity, would never be seen or heard from again. Not in the public form anyway.

Harold would be taken care of. The best of care too. But his name would be stripped of any kind of attachment to the Bureau, and any cases that he had worked on, any cases that he had solved, would all go to someone else for the glory. He hated it, but it was the way that things were done.

When he was left alone in the room with only Emerald and her husband, he asked her if she was all right. When she nodded and sat down, he smiled at her. This certainly ended all the trouble for her, he thought. Bates was no longer going to be trying to chase her down, or bother her about pictures of what he was sure were long dead relatives. Physically or mentally, not for a long time, if ever.

"I'm sorry about this." He nodded at her. "He was becoming troublesome, but he won't be the last, I'm afraid."

"No, there are men out there like him all the time. Thinking that they know better than most. I'm so very sorry that you were trapped into his thinking. It won't happen again with him." She said that she knew that. "I'm glad. If there is ever anything I can do for you and your family, Mrs. Crosby, you just let us know. We, as an agency, we never thought it would come to this. I know you find this hard to believe, but he was a good man. Still is, I think. But things got out of control for him, and he went too far."

"Thank you. And yes, I do believe he was and still is a good man. Just a little obsessive about things." When she stood up, he thought for a moment, a very quick one, that he saw a little person on her shoulder. Blinking several times didn't make the little creature disappear, so he looked at the woman again. "You know, you might see all kinds of things once you open your mind to it." With a sassy wink, she moved to her husband again.

He sat down after the couple left him. Paddy was sure that he'd seen it. And just as sure that he'd not. Standing up, he decided that he wasn't going to think about it, about what he might or might not have seen. No, he wasn't going to become another Bates.

"Not me. Not in this lifetime." He closed his mouth, thinking that talking to himself wasn't going to help either. So, as he made his way to his car, Paddy made sure that he didn't look around. And in doing so, he thought about his life and career, and made a resolution that he was never returning to this town. It didn't matter to him if the entire town became terrorists, which he thought would never happen, but not him. He wasn't coming back. Never ever-ever.

Stopping by to see Nash and his wife seemed a bad idea as well. The sooner he left the better, he told himself. He had cases to clear off his desk, and a report to write. Things would be better once he was home, once he was back to normal. A giggle escaped his lips, and he put his hand over his mouth to stifle any more that might slip by him.

Normal? What the fuck did that even mean anymore?

Before You Go...

HELP AN AUTHOR

write a review

THANK YOU!

Share your voice and help guide other readers to these wonderful books. Even if it's only a line or two your reviews help readers discover the author's books so they can continue creating stories that you'll love. Login to your favorite retailer and leave a review. Thank you.

Kathi Barton, winner of the Pinnacle Book Achievement award as well as a best-selling author on Amazon and All Romance books, lives in Nashport, Ohio with her husband Paul. When not creating new worlds and romance, Kathi and her husband enjoy camping and going to auctions. She can also be seen at county fairs with her husband who is an artist and potter.

Her muse, a cross between Jimmy Stewart and Hugh Jackman, brings her stories to life for her readers in a way that has them coming back time and again for more. Her favorite genre is paranormal romance with a great deal of spice. You can visit Kathi online and drop her an email if you'd like. She loves hearing from her fans. aaronskiss@gmail.com.

Follow Kathi on her blog: http://kathisbartonauthor. blogspot.com/